ARMY I

Two brothers, div...
meet the women who will change ...
for ever!

Army medics Marc and Nick Rousseau
were at the top of their field when they were
caught in an IED explosion in Afghanistan
that left Marc paralysed and Nick unscathed.
Now out of the army, the estranged brothers
are on opposite sides of the country and
struggling to put the past behind them…
until they each meet a woman who
challenges them in unimaginable ways.

Now, as these generous and caring women
open the brothers' eyes to new worlds
of possibility, can Marc and Nick finally
forgive the past and reclaim the bond
they once shared?

Don't miss the ***Army Docs*** duet
by Mills & Boon® Medical Romance™ authors
Dianne Drake and Amy Ruttan

Read Marc and Anne's story in
Tortured by Her Touch

Read Nick and Jennifer's story in
It Happened in Vegas

Available now!

Dear Reader,

Thank you for picking up a copy of *It Happened in Vegas*.

I love writing about brothers—probably because I'm surrounded by them. My mother had three brothers, my dad was the youngest of eight, and there was only one sister right in the middle. I have a younger brother, and my own daughter has two younger brothers.

Brothers—I know them well. I know that the love they share, though not always evident to strangers, is there.

My hero Nick feels he's wronged his brother, Marc, and for that he punishes himself—until both brothers learn to reach out and heal each other. Of course this is done with the help of a good woman by their sides.

Why did I set this story in Vegas? Simply because I love the desert and badlands—there's just something about the wide open spaces, the arid foothills and the landscape which seem so harsh. Nevada is a state that is on top of my bucket list. I hope I get to visit one day.

I hope you enjoy *It Happened in Vegas*.

I love hearing from readers, so please drop by my website, www.amyruttan.com, or give me a shout on Twitter @ruttanamy.

With warmest wishes

Amy Ruttan

IT HAPPENED IN VEGAS

BY
AMY RUTTAN

First published in Great Britain 2015
by Mills & Boon, an imprint of Harlequin (UK) Limited,
Large Print edition 2015
Eton House, 18-24 Paradise Road,
Richmond, Surrey, TW9 1SR

© 2015 Amy Ruttan

ISBN: 978-0-263-25501-0

Harlequin (UK) Limited's policy is to use papers that are natural, renewable and recyclable products and made from wood grown in sustainable forests. The logging and manufacturing processes conform to the legal environmental regulations of the country of origin.

Printed and bound in Great Britain
by CPI Antony Rowe, Chippenham, Wiltshire

Born and raised on the outskirts of Toronto, Ontario, **Amy Ruttan** fled the big city to settle down with the country boy of her dreams. When she's not furiously typing away at her computer she's mom to three wonderful children, who have given her another job as a taxi driver.

A voracious reader, she was given her first romance novel by her grandmother, who shared her penchant for a hot romance. From that moment Amy was hooked by the magical worlds, handsome heroes and sigh-worthy romances contained in the pages, and she knew what she wanted to be when she grew up.

Life got in the way, but after the birth of her second child she decided to pursue her dream of becoming a romance author.

Amy loves to hear from readers. It makes her day, in fact. You can find out more about Amy at her website: www.amyruttan.com

Books by Amy Ruttan

Dare She Date Again?
Pregnant with the Soldier's Son
Melting the Ice Queen's Heart
Safe in His Hands

**Visit the author profile page
at millsandboon.co.uk for more titles**

This book is dedicated to all the brothers
in my life and my plethora of uncles,
in particular two who are no longer with us:
Uncle Jim and Uncle Wavell.
And most especially to my brother Mike.
Sorry for duct taping you to the wall
periodically when we were younger.

PROLOGUE

ANOTHER DINNER PARTY.

Jennifer plastered on another fake smile as she walked around the crowded reception hall in the Nevada State Capitol.

It's for a good cause. It's for a good cause.

And it was. She had nothing against a bill for soldier benefits. She just hated dinner parties like this, endless campaigns, looking good for the press. She knew her father; this wasn't just for the men and women who served their country. This was just because the elections were coming up in a few years and he was eyeing the White House.

It had nothing to do with soldiers.

Not a thing. It was all an image, another empty promise. She really hated politics. It brought out the worst in her father, a man she fondly remembered as being so different.

He hadn't always been this way. She remembered a different father, a loving, caring and *real* man. It was this political side of him she wasn't thrilled with.

Jennifer picked up a flute of champagne and tried to avoid the flash of cameras as reporters flocked around her father. Her perfect sister stood with her parents, smiling and chatting with the press, eating up the attention. The attention brought to her family made her nervous because she hadn't had the best relationship with them since her father had got into the political arena over a decade ago.

She was, after all, the black sheep, which meant the press were constantly dogging her heels. They'd backed off somewhat since she'd become a doctor. A doctor wasn't juicy enough for the paparazzi. Well, it was thrilling enough for her.

She'd rather be in the OR tonight, saving lives, but instead she was here and pretending to be part of the "perfect" family that her father wanted the world to believe they had.

Ha.

No family was perfect, but her father was ashamed of his roots. How he didn't come from a wealthy heritage.

He didn't want anyone to know that he was the illegitimate son of a congressman and an intern. That he'd worked with his hands to better their lives.

Her father only wanted his voters to see how he'd risen like a phoenix from the ashes.

Everything else burned away.

Jennifer swigged back the expensive champagne and then took another one, ignoring the waiter's eyebrow rising as she set her second empty flute back on the tray.

The waiter left before she could take a third.

It was probably for the best, but Jennifer just shook her head and meandered to a safe, dark corner where she could go unnoticed by everyone.

You'd think that accepting a trauma surgeon fellowship on the east coast would be something *most* parents would be proud of, and maybe her father would be, but her perfect sister, Pamela, had managed to become engaged to a high-society socialite from Manhattan and all Jennifer had managed to do was become a surgeon in a hospital.

It was like she had rabies or something.

No matter what she did, she couldn't shake off her past. She couldn't shake off the stigma of being the black sheep in the family.

The one who didn't want to rise from the humble beginnings of her life and mingle with the social elite. She wanted to help the poor and less fortunate.

She fumbled in her purse for the illicit pack of cigarettes, something which she'd been trying desperately to give up since her days as a hellion teen. She'd been off them for a while, but being around her family made her do crazy things.

"Why do you always do things to make me look bad?"

A shudder traveled down her spine as her father's voice whispered in her ear.

Jennifer pushed open the French doors and stepped out into the cool night air. The patio was mostly empty. Everyone was inside, enjoying the party.

There was one sad-looking cigarette in the package. Old and almost crumpled. She pulled it out and turned to toss it away, remembering why she'd quit when she'd started medical school.

It was being around her *perfect* family that made her go bonkers.

She didn't like the act. Couldn't they be real?

"That's not healthy for you, you know that?"

Jennifer spun around and saw that she wasn't alone on the patio. A soldier was half-hidden in the shadows, only three feet from her, sitting on a bench.

He leaned forward and she could see the hazel of his eyes reflected in the moonlight. His face was slim, long, but there was something enticing about it. When he smiled, it was a half-smile that ended in a deep dimple in his left cheek.

"I wasn't going to smoke it. I was going to get rid of it. I quit a long time ago," she said.

The soldier stood slowly and stepped out of the shadows. He was tall, lanky and devilishly appealing in his dress uniform. He whipped off the dress hat and held it under his arm, revealing a buzz cut.

"With all due respect, miss, it appeared that you were ready to devour that cancer stick."

Jennifer chuckled and glanced at the cigarette in her fingers. "Okay, I thought about it, but only for a moment."

He stepped closer and took the cigarette from her hand, snapped it in half and tossed it over the side of the patio into the bushes. "There, the temptation is gone."

"Hey, that's littering. You do realize that, don't you?"

He placed his hat back on his head and raised an ebony eyebrow. "Are you the litter police?"

"No, but you're a soldier. You should know better, hooah and all that."

This time he grinned and his white teeth gleamed in the darkness. "Hooah and all that?"

Jennifer laughed. "Sorry, I don't know. I'm on edge."

"And I just threw away your only means of escape?"

A blush tinged her cheeks. "Something like that."

"Well, my apologies, but I would hate to have you ruin your years of abstinence by lighting up tonight."

"I thank you for your concern, soldier. I do." She snapped her clutch closed. "Shouldn't you be getting back to the party?"

He shrugged. "It's not my thing, too many people. What about you?"

"What about me?" she asked.

He leaned in and a tingle zinged down her spine. "What're you escaping from?"

Don't let him get to you.

She was a sucker for men in uniform, men out of uniform and bad boys in general. All the types of men her parents didn't approve of.

Of course, the only men her parents approved of were from money, high society or a WASP. Also known as her sister's fiancé.

Jennifer cleared her throat and tucked an errant strand of hair behind her ear.

"Oh, I've made you uncomfortable."

"How do you know?"

"You're fidgeting. Admit it, you're nervous around me."

"A bit, but you're right. I'm escaping. I'm not really into shindigs like this."

"Want to get out of here?"

"Uh, you're a complete stranger."

"I'm a soldier, though. Doesn't that make me honorable or something?"

"Not really." She grinned. "I'm Jennifer." And she stuck out her hand.

He took her hand in his and the touch of his skin sent a jolt of heat through her blood.

"I'm Nick. I guess we're not strangers any longer?"

"Nope. We're not. What was that you were saying about getting out of here?"

He held out his arm. "I hope you don't mind riding a motorcycle."

"I don't mind in the least."

Nick turned to lead her back in through the party and she pulled him back. "What's wrong? Are you having second thoughts?"

"No, I just don't want to go back in there." She didn't want some tabloid to snap a picture of her on the arm of a soldier. Not because it was bad, but because it was an invasion of her privacy, something she held dear because it was the only thing she could control.

He looked around. "Well, can you think of a better way out of here?"

"Hold this." She jammed her clutch into his hands and kicked off her heels.

"What're you doing?"

She smiled. "What, you've never jumped a fence, soldier?"

Jennifer picked up her shoes and tossed them out onto the dark lawn and then climbed the patio fence, dropping down three feet onto the grass below. "Are you coming?"

His answer was to drop her purse at her feet. She scrambled out of the way, retrieving her shoes as he dropped down beside her.

"How did you know to do that?" he asked.

Jennifer panicked. She didn't want him to know who she really was. If he knew she was a senator's daughter, he might not want to "escape" with her.

"It was obvious," she said, brushing it off like it was nothing. "Now, you have to provide the adventure."

He smiled again, that half-smile that brought out that delectable dimple. "Oh, I can provide the adventure. Like I said, my bike is parked down the street."

"Lead the way, soldier."

He took her hand and they ran across the lawn and out onto the street where his motorcycle was sitting. He opened up his pannier and tossed her a helmet as he put his hat safely away and then grabbed his own helmet.

"You carry two helmets? How fortuitous." She crammed it down over her head.

Nick took her purse from her hand and put it in the pannier next to his hat. "Well, I like to come prepared for adventure."

He shut the pannier and climbed on. She sat behind him, gripping him about the waist.

"You're being reckless. You're such an embarrassment."

The words had stung. Like a slap to her face. Her father had never spoken to her like that before, when he'd been a rancher.

Jennifer shook her father's words from her head as Nick started the engine, kicked the stand and took off, heading west out of Carson City.

She didn't know where they were going and she didn't care.

She knew that any rational female wouldn't go off with a man she'd just met, but something deep down inside her trusted him, probably when she shouldn't.

Jennifer didn't even freak when they left Carson City far behind them and headed into the state park.

After almost thirty minutes of driving, he pulled over at the Sand Harbor Overlook in Lake Tahoe State Park.

She let go of her hold on him and got off. Her legs felt a bit shaky, not used to riding on a motorcycle.

"What a great spot," she said as she took off the helmet, handing it back to him. He'd taken his off, too, and set the helmets on the seat.

"Yeah, I love it here. I was planning on coming here after the party. One last look, you could say." There was a hint of sadness in his voice.

"Are you heading overseas?"

Nick nodded. "My tour of duty is two years."

Disappointment gnawed at her.

Damn.

Not that she'd been expecting this to go anywhere, but she was disappointed that they would only have this time together, because once she finished her fellowship at the end of this summer, she could get a job anywhere. Or even stay in Boston. The possibilities were endless.

"See, now you feel all bad for me. Don't. I

serve my country and I'm glad to do it. I also plan to be back to see this lake again."

Jennifer smiled. "Are you from around here originally?"

Nick shook his head. "No, but I've been stationed out this way for a year. Nevada grew on me. I don't think I want to be anywhere else."

He walked down toward the sandy beach through the tall pines, which sighed in the light summer breeze. It made her feel a little cold and she was regretting the sleeveless shift dress she'd chosen to wear.

The sky was bright, full of stars and a large moon was hovering over the lake. A large, bright moon that was reflected in the clear, calm water.

Nick stood on the beach, gazing up at the moon. He'd taken off his dress jacket and laid it on a large boulder. He was unbuttoning the shirt, his sleeves already rolled up to his elbows.

"You're not planning to swim, are you?" Jennifer teased.

He looked back at her over his shoulder and winked. "Maybe. Are you up for skinny-dipping?"

Jennifer chuckled. "Ah, no. It's cold. Especially

here. That water can't be any more than fifty degrees."

Nick frowned and glanced at the water. "You think so?"

"I know so."

He looked at her. "So you're native to this area?"

"Yeah," she said, but with hardly any enthusiasm. It wasn't that she didn't like Nevada. As a child, she'd loved it. She'd loved northern Nevada, everything about it. The desert, the mountains and plains.

And she'd loved the Lake Tahoe area.

When she'd been younger, her father had had a ranch outside Carson City. They'd been so happy there, but then her father had sold it when she was ten. He'd told them he had bigger aspirations for all of them and he wasn't going to waste his life grubbing away on a ranch.

So, yeah, she loved Nevada.

It was just her father, the notoriety that went with being his daughter. She wanted to escape all that. In Boston, she wasn't the senator's daughter. She was Dr. Mills. Trauma fellow.

She didn't like being in the limelight. She

didn't like being the black-sheep daughter, afraid to breathe the wrong way, worried that it would ruin her father's political career, seeing her face plastered on the local newspapers.

A splash and a shout distracted her from those thoughts.

Nick was wading in the shallow water. "Man, that is cold!"

Jennifer couldn't help but laugh. "I told you."

"Woo, so cold. Why don't you come and try it out?"

Jennifer shook her head, but couldn't stop laughing.

"You know, I never pegged you for a chicken." He was teasing her, egging her on. She knew it.

"I'm not chicken. I've been in Lake Tahoe before. I know *exactly* how cold it is."

Nick glanced down at his feet. "You know, it's not too bad. You get used to it."

Jennifer rolled her eyes and kicked off her heels. "It's probably because your body is succumbing to hypothermia."

Nick grinned. "Come on in. Just wade. I'm not brave enough to go swimming."

"I'm coming." She lifted her dress and undid

the clasps on her garter belt to peel off her stockings, and when she glanced over at Nick, she could see his gaze transfixed on her legs. He was watching her roll down her stockings.

It caused her blood to heat, the thought of him watching her, knowing he was undressing her in his mind.

What am I doing?

Having fun, letting loose and living the way you used to live.

Living like everyone did.

Once she was free, she walked down to the water's edge and grimaced. "I can feel the chill from here."

"Come on in, you sissy." Nick bent down and sent a gentle splash in her direction. "People up north do this all the time."

"Yeah, well, people up north might be addled by the cold weather."

Nick chucked. "Think of it like a polar-bear dip."

She took a deep breath and waded into the water, which was frigid and bit at her skin like knives. "Oh, my God. You're insane."

Jennifer turned to leave, but he was over to her

in a flash, wrapping his arms around her waist and stopping her from leaving. They were so close she could smell his cologne. It was a clean scent, but there was something else she couldn't put her finger on. Whatever it was, it was making her feel faint.

His arms around her were so strong, steadying her.

She glanced up and his hazel eyes twinkled from the reflection of the water and the moonlight. He reached up and stroked her face, his thumb brushing against the apple of her cheek, and she turned her face into his touch instinctively.

"Can I ask you a boon?" he said, his voice deep and husky.

"A boon? Have I suddenly been transported back in time?" she teased.

Nick grinned. "A favor, then, for a soldier who's about to leave on a *long* tour of duty. I wouldn't normally ask this of a woman I'd just met, but this has always kind of been a fantasy of mine."

"What?" she asked, the butterflies in her stomach swirling around.

Nick leaned forward and whispered in her ear, "A kiss, in the moonlight."

A tingle raced down her spine. She didn't know what to expect, wasn't sure what she was willing to give him. A kiss seemed doable but, then, the way he was affecting her, the way she was feeling, being so free and standing in freezing-cold water with a stranger and wanting to do more than just kiss him…

He was going on a tour of duty and she was heading back to Boston to finish off her fellowship. Their paths would probably never cross again.

There were no expectations and when she looked back on this moment in the future, she could look on it with the fondness of something romantic she'd done, instead of looking on it with regret that she hadn't taken the chance, because something deep down inside her was telling her, screaming at her to take the chance.

"I think I can accommodate that request."

Nick smiled. "I'm so glad you said that."

She closed her eyes as he moved closer. She didn't know what to expect because kissing had never been her favorite aspect of physical contact.

Every time she'd been kissed before had been less than stellar.

When his lips brushed across hers, lightly, she knew that this was a kiss she'd been waiting for, she just hadn't known it. Until now.

His hands cradled her head gently, his fingers in her hair. He pulled her body closer so she was flush against him as his kiss deepened, making her weak in the knees.

Nick's hands moved from her face and down her back. The feeling of his hands on her, on the small bit of exposed flesh on her back, made her blood heat.

The kiss ended, much to her dismay, but Nick still held her and her arms were still around his neck as they stood in the shallow water of Lake Tahoe.

Jennifer took a deep breath. "I…I'd better get going."

Nick smiled at her. That lazy half-smile that made her heart flutter. "Really? You want to go."

Yes.

"No. No, I don't."

He bent down and scooped her up in his arms. "Good." That was all he said as he carried her to shore.

CHAPTER ONE

Three years later

"I THINK YOU'LL be very happy here as our head of trauma."

Jennifer smiled politely at the chief of surgery, Dr. Ramsgate, as they walked the halls of the hospital.

"All Saints Hospital is one of the top hospitals in Las Vegas, and with our new trauma wing opening soon…" Dr. Ramsgate continued and Jennifer tuned him out, only because she knew all the benefits of All Saints Hospital—it's what had attracted her to this facility above all others in Nevada. The new trauma ward under construction would be the most modern in the country.

And her father was happy she'd returned to Nevada in time for his campaigning.

How good would it look if his surgeon daughter was working in her home state? Only Jennifer hadn't come home for her father.

She'd come home to lick her wounds after her cardiothoracic fiancé had jilted her and then stolen the research they'd worked on together, before marrying someone else. There was no way she was going to remain in the same hospital in Boston with him, let alone the same state.

She'd moved back to be near her family. To hide from the humiliation. To remember why she'd become a surgeon.

Even if it had meant turning down a job at a prestigious Minnesota clinic.

At least it's warmer in Las Vegas.

So that was a plus. She wouldn't miss the winters.

Jennifer had had to get back to her roots and, most important, she was going to keep away from men. Especially other male surgeons.

She wasn't going to make that mistake twice.

"And here's our current trauma department. It's not much, but it's served us well." Dr. Ramsgate was waiting for her to say something. "Of course, once the new wing is complete, this will close."

"It's wonderful. It's laid out well." It was a minor fib as she hadn't really even looked at it, but a quick scan told her she wasn't being totally false. It *was* laid out well. It was open and had lots of trauma rooms, with easy access to get gurneys in and out. Though the new trauma department would be better.

The ER was quiet for the moment, though she was sure that could change on a moment's notice, like so many trauma departments.

She was eager to get this walk-through over and done with so she could throw on some scrubs, a yellow isolation gown and get her hands dirty. Figuratively, of course.

Until then, she had to play nice with the chief of surgery.

"Come, I'll introduce you to the staff on duty before we head back upstairs to finish your paperwork." Dr. Ramsgate motioned to the charge desk, where a surgeon stood with his back to them. Jennifer's brow furrowed, because the surgeon leaning over the desk charting tugged at the foggy corners of her mind.

There was something familiar about his stance.

"Dr. Rousseau, this is Dr. Mills, the new head of trauma."

The surgeon standing at the desk turned to greet her and when she came face to face with him, the foggy memory that had been eluding her came rushing back, like a tsunami of the senses. It was an overload in her brain, the way it had happened.

Lake Tahoe, a brilliant moon, starry sky and a whispered request brushing against her ear that still made her body zing with anticipation even years later.

"A kiss, in the moonlight."

It had been three years and she wondered if he remembered her. He'd changed and so had she. His buzz cut had grown out, but his ebony hair was trimmed and well kept. There was stubble on his face, but it suited him. Even more than the clean-shaven face.

And a scar ran down his left cheek and she couldn't help but wonder if it came from his time overseas. There was no wedding ring on his finger, but that didn't mean anything. He might've come from surgery and taken it off.

His hazel eyes widened for just a moment, then

he held out his hand. "It's a pleasure to meet you, Dr. Mills."

"The pleasure is all mine, Dr. Rousseau."

Dr. Ramsgate nodded, pleased. "Well, we'll let you get back to work, Dr. Rousseau. I have much more to show you, Dr. Mills."

Jennifer found it harder to breathe, her pulse was thundering in her ears like an out-of-control high-speed train and it was like she was going to derail right here in the emergency room.

Dr. Rousseau nodded, but didn't tear his gaze from hers until Dr. Ramsgate stepped between them, breaking the connection. If there even was one. Maybe she was losing her mind a bit.

What had happened between them had only been a fleeting moment.

"Dr. Mills, are you ready? I'd like to introduce you to some of the other staff members you'll be in charge of." Confusion was etched across Dr. Ramsgate's face at her absentmindedness.

"Yes, of course." She fell into step beside Dr. Ramsgate, though not without stealing a quick look over her shoulder at the charge desk, but Dr. Rousseau had disappeared; evaporated like he'd been nothing more than a figment of her imagination.

Only he wasn't.

He wasn't a foggy piece of a memory. One that she only allowed herself to think of from time to time. The one perfect romantic moment she'd had in her life. That soldier hadn't left her standing at an altar, hadn't stolen her work, and the kiss he'd given her still made her blood heat. Even after all this time.

This was going to be bad.

She had no inclination to allow her heart to open again, especially to another surgeon.

Jennifer knew she'd have to avoid Dr. Nick Rousseau and that wasn't going to be an easy thing. Especially now she was in charge of his department.

She was in serious trouble.

Nick put the chart back in the filing cabinet. He'd moved away from the charge desk when Dr. Ramsgate had stepped between them, breaking the connection between him and Jennifer. It had been the escape he'd needed.

He wasn't sure if Jennifer remembered him,

from the look on her face. Maybe he just looked familiar to her, someone she couldn't place. Which was fine. It was good she didn't remember him, but he certainly remembered her.

There was no way he could forget that night.

Not when it was burned into his brain.

Not when every time he'd closed his eyes for the last three years he'd been able to feel the silky softness of her skin under his fingertips, inhale the fruity scent of her hair and taste the sweetness of her lips.

Though that's all that had happened.

Just a kiss.

Well, several kisses, but it had been all he'd needed to carry him through his long tour of duty. When he'd been working at the front line, patching up soldiers, saving lives and, yes, even when one thoughtless act of bravery had cost his own brother dearly.

Nick clenched his fist and shook those thoughts away.

No, he wouldn't think about Marc and he wouldn't think about his brother hating him right now, because he couldn't let those emotions out to air. When he thought of that moment, he hated himself. He'd let his anger get the better of him.

There was already talk circulating around the hospital about him, about his rages and about how he'd put his fist through a window once.

He was doing better. Or he thought he was.

Maybe it was seeing her again—whatever it was, it shook him. He'd been surprised to learn she was a surgeon.

That night they'd spent on the beach, talking to each other, she'd never told him that she was a physician, in particular a trauma surgeon.

Then again, he'd never opened up about why he was going overseas on his tour of duty. He hadn't told her that he was an army medic.

She'd changed, but not so much that he hadn't recognized her. The long blond hair was gone. She sported a pixie cut, which still suited her. It gave him a better view of her long, slender neck and he knew that if he kissed that spot under her ear she sighed with pleasure.

Don't think about that.

Nick stifled a groan and left the charting area and headed toward the doctors' lounge to get a cup of coffee.

He didn't have time to date and had no interest in it.

After all, he was too irresponsible for any kind of settled life.

At least, that's what Marc had always said. And, frankly, Nick didn't deserve to be happy. Solitude was his penance for what he'd done.

After the accident that had paralyzed his brother and left him unscathed, he'd finished his tour of duty with an honorable discharge. Though there was nothing honorable in his mind.

If he hadn't tried to run out when the medic unit had been under fire to save his buddy, Marc never would've followed him.

And though he'd saved his friend and was deemed a hero, the IED had exploded, paralyzing Marc, leaving Nick without a brother.

Not that Marc had died, but he'd cut Nick out of his life. It was like Marc was dead. Nick was definitely dead to Marc.

He was a ghost.

So Nick had left him alone, like Marc wanted. He hadn't returned home to Chicago. He'd settled in Nevada. In the place he'd last remembered being happy. With the vast, open desert plains and the mountains and foothills to the north, a man could get lost.

And he was lost. His parents didn't speak with him and neither did his sister. Marc needed them more anyway.

Here in Las Vegas, a man could be forgotten and maybe he'd be able to shake the ghosts of his past.

He just hadn't expected he'd run into one of them.

Jennifer had never told him she was a surgeon and he'd thought she was in Carson City, which was on the other side of the state, six hours away.

Then her name rang more bells.

Jennifer Mills.

She'd been at that state dinner thrown by Senator Mills. Was she his daughter? The one who'd been jilted? He didn't know much about it because he didn't really care about gossip columns. Heck, he didn't even have cable. Jennifer had her own cross to bear and he wouldn't pry.

Nick scrubbed his hand over his face. Dammit. She was off-limits for sure. Senator Mills had been the one to present him with his Medal of Honor for bravery. One that he kept hidden away under his socks because he didn't deserve it; especially after what had happened to Marc.

He was no hero.

He was irresponsible. Always getting into scrapes, and Marc had always been there to bail him out.

Now Marc wasn't there for him anymore.

Even though Nick's wanderlust and sense of adventure still ate away at him, he didn't feed the beast.

He just wanted to work. To be the best damn surgeon he could be. Maybe to show his brother he wasn't reckless and irresponsible.

Jennifer's appearance complicated things.

Nick poured himself a cup of coffee. The thought that she'd been involved with someone else made him feel a bit jealous.

Though he had no claim on her.

They'd only exchanged first names. They'd only shared a few passionate kisses under the stars.

He could work with her. Not that he had a choice, because in Las Vegas he was a nobody.

He wasn't a hero, he wasn't a soldier. He was

just a face in the crowd and that's the way he liked it.

Nick slouched down in a chair, leaning his head against the low back to close his eyes for just a moment.

The door slammed and he sat up. Jennifer had entered, and pink tinged her cheeks when she saw him sitting there. He liked the way she blushed; she'd blushed like that against the sand when he'd kissed her.

"Sorry, Dr. Rousseau. I hope I didn't wake you."

"I wasn't asleep, Dr. Mills. I thought you were with Dr. Ramsgate?"

"He had a quick cardio consult and he told me I could get a cup of coffee in here." She nervously brushed at her hair, tucking the short strands behind her delicate ear, like she'd done when they'd first met. Only there were no more long strands.

She moved over to the coffeemaker and poured herself a cup, then proceeded to stand there, staring at the bulletin board, which was full of ads of stuff for sale and take-out menus. Just junk. She fidgeted with her hair again.

Nick could sense she felt uncomfortable. The

tension was thick in the air. He knew the feeling of a standoff. The calm before the storm.

"You can have a seat. I don't bite and you should know that."

Jennifer spun around and frowned. "You do remember me, you dingbat."

Nick couldn't help but chuckle. "Dingbat?"

"I don't curse much. I try not to…"

"Dingbat isn't cursing. Now, the F word, that's cursing."

She winced. "Why did you act like you hadn't met me?"

Nick cocked an eyebrow. "You did the same thing!"

"I thought you were a soldier." She sat down in the chair across from him.

"I was. I was an army medic."

"You never told me that." A smile played around her kissable lips.

"Ah, we're going to play that game, eh? Well, you never exactly told me that you were a surgeon, or a senator's daughter, for that matter."

She blushed again. "Fine. You have me, but I would really appreciate it if you wouldn't spread around the fact I'm a senator's daughter."

"Is your father crooked?" he teased.

Jennifer's eyes narrowed. "Hardly. I just don't want the notoriety to follow me. I'm a damn good trauma surgeon. I don't want that to cloud my team's judgment of me. I *earned* my reputation."

Nick nodded. "Of course."

"Good." She bit her bottom lip. "Well, I'd better see if Dr. Ramsgate is through. It's good to see you again, Dr. Rousseau. I'm glad no harm came to you overseas."

Nick didn't respond as she got up and left the doctors' lounge.

"I'm glad no harm came to you overseas."

Even though she'd truly meant it, it still stung.

He touched the scar on his face. The only injury he'd sustained when the IED had blown.

Could his brother say the same? His brother had been sent home a year early, had had to leave the service.

Nick got to finish out his tour of duty.

Nick could still walk, run and keep up with the fast pace of trauma.

Marc couldn't.

So, no, he hadn't come back home unharmed.

Nick crushed the empty coffee cup in his hand

and tossed it into the trash. Crushing the cup in his hand sated his ire, but only just. There was only one thing he could do to control this—he was going to bury himself in his work.

He was going to forget that stolen moment on Lake Tahoe with Jennifer, because he didn't deserve that kind of happiness.

Nick was going to be the best surgeon he could be and maybe then his brother would think better of him and nothing, not even a woman, was going to distract him.

He couldn't let it.

CHAPTER TWO

JENNIFER WAS GLAD to get all the paperwork and HR stuff done in enough time to head down to the ER and actually practice some medicine. She hadn't had a chance to do any in a month, what with trying to find another job and moving across the country after her ex-fiancé had published the research they'd shared and been given a promotion at her old hospital in Boston.

She'd planned to stick it out. After all, he'd jilted her the previous year. She'd held her own and had faced him every day because she'd refused to be bullied out of the career she'd built, but then, when she'd let her guard down, he'd betrayed her.

The hospital board had backed him. After all, he'd been a surgical rock star, a god in their eyes, and he'd bring in lots of money.

Jennifer had been a nobody, as far as they

were concerned. Just an easy, replaceable trauma surgeon.

So she'd given them the proverbial finger and left, leaving their trauma department to be run by a moron.

All Saints Hospital in Las Vegas had offered her everything to come and run their trauma department. And they were building a state-of-the-art facility better than that at Boston Mercy. So that was a plus. Even though it felt like she was returning home with her tail between her legs, she wasn't. No, she was going to make All Saints Hospital shine like a star, like a supernova.

She smiled to herself as she slipped on the disposable yellow isolation gown over her dark green scrubs. The dark green scrubs marked her as an attending, while the interns and residents ran around in orange.

Jennifer shuddered. It wasn't even a nice orange. Maybe she could have a talk with the chief about changing the color scheme of scrubs at the hospital.

Why the heck are you thinking about color schemes at a time like this?

She sighed. She didn't need to be having this

weird internal dialogue with herself. Ever since David had jilted her, people hadn't treated her the same. They'd pitied her and she'd retreated a bit into her head.

That was another reason she'd had to get away. Though she knew the people at All Saints knew about her past. She could see it in their eyes, but she didn't care. She was going to hold her head high.

She was not some screwball, crazy, jilted-bride-type person. She was a surgeon. A fine one.

No. A damn good one.

A neutron star.

Okay, your obsession with astronomy really needs to stop now.

"Dr. Mills, the ambulance is seven minutes out!" a nurse shouted as Jennifer walked into the triage area.

"Thanks." She headed outside to the tarmac to await the arrival of the ambulance, craning her head, listening for the distant wail. It was a quirk of hers to know exactly how far away an ambulance was by the siren. Only with All

Saints being right near the strip, Jennifer couldn't drown out the rest of the noise to hear anything.

"What do we have coming in?"

She spun around to see Dr. Rousseau in an isolation gown standing next to her.

Damn.

"I thought you were on a break, as in napping in the on-call room?"

"Disappointed that I'm not?"

Jennifer rolled her eyes. "Hardly, but I heard it's something minor. Something coming from one of the casinos. It's probably just a myocardial infarction. You know, too much excitement at the slots."

Nick cocked an eyebrow. "Oh, I think it's something a bit more than a minor myocardial infarction. Though I doubt you could call any myocardial infarction minor."

"You know something. Don't you?" she asked, scrutinizing him. "What do you know?"

"If you don't know, I'm not going to tell you. I want to see the look of surprise on your face when the ambulance comes in."

"That's unprofessional."

Nick grinned. "Hey, it's Vegas and what happens in Vegas…"

"Stays in Vegas. I know. I'm from Nevada." She crossed her arms and stared up at the sky. The buildings from the strip loomed from behind the back of a casino. You could see the top of the Eiffel Tower if you craned your head a certain way.

"It's priceless. Trust me. It's a great initiation."

"I'm the head of trauma. We're not supposed to be initiated or hazed."

Nick shrugged. "Come on. It's fun. Think of it as a morale booster."

Jennifer was going to say a few more choice words when the ambulance came roaring up. The paramedic jumped out and opened the back door.

"Jack Palmer, a twelve-year-old male who has a three-inch laceration to his forehead."

As the paramedics were bringing down the stretcher, Jennifer leaned over to Nick. "How is a three-inch lac supposed to be an initiation?"

Nick just grinned. "You'll see."

The little boy groaned as the stretcher was placed on the ground. His head was bandaged, there was blood coming through the gauze and the boy was hiccuping between groans. Jennifer stepped beside it and heard a tinny hum of "Happy Birthday."

"What's that noise?"

Jack hiccuped. "It's my birthday card."

"Where is it? I can hold your birthday card for you." Jennifer looked on the gurney, while a paramedic was stifling a chuckle and Nick was grinning from ear to ear like a Cheshire cat.

"No, you can't." Jack hiccuped again.

"Why not?"

Jack shook his head and his face flushed. Jennifer looked at the female paramedic. "What's going on?"

"The card is the reason he got the head injury. He swallowed the music player from the card."

Jennifer's eyes widened and she looked down at the patient. "What?"

Nick signed off on the patient and the paramedics mumbled "Good luck" before leaving. Jennifer and Nick wheeled the boy inside.

When they got Jack in a triage room with the door shut, he hiccuped again, playing that annoying tune. Jennifer turned away residents because it was just a simple head lac and as Jack was obviously embarrassed about his situation, she wanted to give him some privacy. For the time being, anyway. The news would get around the hospital and she would need to take a couple of residents in when she surgically removed it.

What happens in Vegas stays in Vegas.

"Jack, please tell me the paramedics are joking."

"Would I be here if they were?" Jack winced again, hiccuped another verse of "Happy Birthday." "Darn."

"How did this happen?" she asked.

"It was a dare. I swallowed it, choked and hit my head on the table."

"Order a CT scan. Stat," Jennifer said to Nick.

"I'm on it," Nick said, rushing out of the room.

"They're all going to laugh at me now. Aren't they?" Jack asked.

"No one is going to laugh at you, Jack. Not on my watch." Though it was very hard not to laugh just a little, but she kept it together. She peeled off the gauze and began to inspect the head wound, getting it ready to clean and stitch.

Nick had the feeling he was being watched. Intently. He had a sixth sense about when he was being watched. Actually, when he was being studied.

"More suction, please," Nick said to the intern who was working with him.

"Yes, Dr. Rousseau."

It was in that brief moment when the intern was suctioning that Nick snuck a glance up at the gallery. There was only one person in the gallery, watching his routine appendectomy, and that was Jennifer.

Not Jennifer. Don't call her by her first name. She's your boss.

She was Dr. Mills.

Only he couldn't think of her as Dr. Mills. She was Jennifer, and he watched her sitting in the gallery, watching his surgery, her arms crossed in a very serious pose.

So different from when they'd been on the beach at Lake Tahoe.

What he wouldn't give to be back there again. Right now.

Then again, that was a dangerous thought.

One he didn't particularly want to think about because he couldn't indulge it, and he *so* wanted to indulge it, which was bad.

Nick tore his gaze away from her and focused back on the appendectomy. He tried to ignore the fact she was in the gallery. He'd known there was someone in there, watching him. Other surgeons and interns had watched him before. It didn't faze him, but the moment he'd glanced up into that gallery and seen it was her, it was different.

And it irked him.

Why was she affecting him so much?

Maybe he shouldn't have flirted with her, but he couldn't help himself when he was around her. It was like he lost all control.

And control was important.

Control meant that he wouldn't act before he thought.

That behavior in the past had been disastrous for him. He just had to look at Marc to remind himself of that daily.

"Don't go out there. Are you crazy?"

"I have to, he's my friend. I'll be okay." Nick *ignored his brother's arguments and ran out into the fray. Bullets whizzed past him, his brother screaming his name behind him.*

Nick forced himself to focus as he pulled on

the purse strings and inverted the stump into the cecum. He couldn't think about that right now.

"Your recklessness cost you your brother." Those had been the last words his father had said to him.

When he thought of that moment, he became angry. He lost control.

So he couldn't let Jennifer into his head.

When he did, he lost the control that he fought so hard to maintain. He was a respected surgeon. He did his job well.

His anger wouldn't get the better of him.

No one's life was in danger and the window-smashing had been a one-off. He rolled his shoulders, tension creeping up his spine. He had to get out of there.

"Why don't you close, Dr. Murphy?" Nick said to his resident as he stepped away from the patient.

Dr. Murphy handed his clamp to a nurse and moved around to finish off the appendectomy as Nick walked toward the scrub room, with one last look up at the gallery.

Jennifer wasn't there anymore. She'd left.

He was going to have to try to avoid her. It was for the best.

Of course, he'd said that to himself before, and what had he done? He'd thrown her an interesting case, to watch her reaction. The patient had probably been one of the first of the interesting cases she'd see, working in the trauma department of All Saints Hospital.

He could've taken that case instead of surprising her with it.

Once he'd realized how much he'd been enjoying the banter with her, he'd left the room. Left her to deal with the patient on her own and found his own case.

An emergency appendectomy.

He pulled off his soiled gown, tossed it in the laundry bin and threw the gloves in the waste receptacle before heading to the sink.

"Thank you for that."

Nick glanced over his shoulder and stepped on the bar under the sink, turning on the water so he could scrub.

"For what?" he asked, feigning innocence, though he was anything but. He knew exactly what she was talking about.

"You know very well."

Nick shook the excess water into the sink and grabbed a towel. "I thought you deserved an interesting case on your first day."

Jennifer raised an eyebrow. "Swallowing part of a birthday card isn't very interesting."

"How can you say that? He serenaded you with every hiccup."

She pinched the bridge of her nose. "It was an annoying song."

"How many of those have you seen?"

"None."

Nick shrugged. "Then I don't really see the argument. You got an interesting case."

"Which I promptly passed on to a resident to retrieve through an endoscope."

"You gave it up?" Nick gasped.

Jennifer just rolled her eyes and walked away from him.

Just let her go.

Only he couldn't. He followed her. "I can't believe you gave it to your resident."

"It was easy for my resident to do."

"I gave you an interesting surgery. You could've had my appendectomy instead." He fell into step beside her. "I could've kept it."

Jennifer snorted. "I wish you had. As it is, Dr. Fallon is an excellent surgical resident and I'm sure I left the patient in capable hands."

"I'm sure you did."

Jennifer stopped and turned to face him. "You did well in there. I mean, I didn't have a good view way up in the gallery, but you have a good touch with your interns and residents in the OR."

Her admiration, her praise pleased him. A lot of people had avoided him since his mishap when he'd first arrived. It's why he was known as a lone wolf, though he wasn't. Not really.

Nick nodded. "Thank you for your professional appraisal. Is that why you came to the gallery?"

She hesitated and tucked a wisp of hair behind her ear. "Of course. Why else would I come?"

Nick didn't believe her for one second. He didn't know her well, but he knew when someone was lying. It was a sort of superpower of his, and she was lying.

"I thought you wanted to call me out on the carpet for a swallowed birthday card."

Her brow furrowed and a flicker of a smile played across her pink, kissable lips.

Get a hold on yourself. Stop thinking about them as kissable.

"It did keep playing the music over and over. I hope his birthday wasn't totally ruined. However, my appearance in the gallery was because I'm evaluating all my trauma surgeons."

"Should I be worried?"

She smiled slyly. "Is there a reason why you should be worried?"

Nick chuckled. *Run. Turn and run.*

Tension hovered between them and he longed to kiss her again. All he had to do was reach out and touch her. Put his arm around her and bring her close to him, pull her against his body and—

His pager went off before he even had a chance to do anything. *Saved by the bell.*

"Let's go, Dr. Rousseau." Jennifer held up her pager. "Large trauma coming in."

She pushed past him and ran down the hall.

Avoiding her was harder than he thought.

He was doomed.

Jennifer watched him work across the ER. A large pileup on the interstate had flooded the hospital with crash victims. Thankfully, there were no *interesting* cases. Just regular trauma—not that it was good, but at least she could scrub in instead of having residents fish music makers out of kids' stomachs.

She'd gone to the gallery to call him out, but then she'd watched him do the appendectomy. Had seen how he'd taught his residents and interns. He'd been so calm and the fluid motion of his hands as he'd inverted the stump had been pure poetry.

Her ex-fiancé wouldn't have lowered himself to do an appendectomy. Even though he was a cardiothoracic surgeon, an appendectomy was beneath him. Best left to the general surgeons and residents.

Appendectomies were easy. What he'd wanted had been the high-profile cases. The cases that would get him the press coverage, would give him the glory.

When she'd first met David, she'd admired his drive and she'd swooned when he'd paid her attention. He'd made her feel like a princess, but all she had been was a trophy, and when he'd found something brighter, something shinier, she'd been dropped.

David had got what he'd wanted from her. The publicity, the research and her heart.

Nick seemed to revel in simplicity. Or at least that's what she got from watching his surgery, his easygoing attitude, but he was guarded.

There was a wall there, one he used flirting to hide, but he was keeping people out. In her brief time talking to other staff members, they'd said he was a bit of a loner. Kept to himself, ate his lunch alone and not many people knew much about him.

The only conversations he engaged in were medical. Case files, papers. The only other thing the staff knew about him was that he had served in the military and been decorated. Something about bravery, but no one knew for sure.

There was also an incident about him getting angry with another surgeon and smashing a window in the doctors' lounge. Anger issues, which had been swept under the rug. It had happened so soon after his return from overseas that people had given him the benefit of the doubt, but for the most part the staff stayed away from him.

Jennifer would've never pegged him to have anger issues.

Everything about him was a mystery.

And she couldn't help but wonder why.

Don't wonder. Just keep away.

It was for the best. She was here to work. To be a surgeon. She didn't need or want love.

When the hubbub of the ER died down and she was scrubbing out of surgery, she saw Nick again. He was rushing down the hall, his surgical gown billowing out behind him as he pushed a gurney to Recovery.

He was a mystery man and she had a thing for mystery men.

Damn.

She glanced at the clock. She still had six hours left on her shift and it was now after midnight. She really needed to get some sleep.

Jennifer headed to the nearest on-call room and collapsed on a cot. As she lay down, she glanced at the nightstand and saw a medical journal.

"Oh, you've got to be kidding me." She picked up the magazine and stared at the grinning face of the man who'd left her standing in a white puffy dress while the press had snapped thousands of pictures of the disgraced, heartbroken and jilted senator's daughter.

The journal was touting Dr. David Morgan's medical breakthrough and how he was up for an award for excellence.

With a *tsk* of disgust and rage, she tossed it at the door just as it was opening, thus beaning Nick in the head, right between the eyes.

She held her breath, hoping he wouldn't get angry with her. Instead, he rubbed his forehead and bent to pick up the magazine.

"Uh, is this your way of telling me you want me to read more medical journals?" He glanced down at the cover. "Ah, I've been meaning to read this one. I'm eager to read all about the Morgan method for aortic dissections."

Jennifer kept her snort to herself and rolled over in the cot. "If you don't mind, I'd like to catch about thirty minutes of sleep before I'm paged again."

The door shut and the room went dark, but she knew she wasn't alone as she heard him move across the room and the mattress creak across the way.

The room was silent, and even though she was dog tired, she couldn't sleep knowing that he was across the room. Lying there, all mysterious and handsome, and she knew he was a good kisser. She'd experienced it firsthand.

Damn.

"Are there any private on-call rooms in this hospital?" she asked.

"Nope." Nick yawned. "Is my presence disturbing you?"

"No, I just don't know if you're a snorer or not. I'm a light sleeper."

"I don't snore. Now, if you don't mind, I've been up for twelve hours." The mattress creaked again as he moved.

"Good." She rolled back over and closed her eyes, trying to will herself to fall asleep, but it wasn't working.

"You know, of all the ways I imagined us sleeping together, this wasn't how I envisioned it."

Jennifer's cheeks heated. "Excuse me?"

There was a chuckle in the darkness.

"What's so funny?" Jennifer asked.

"I get under your skin, don't I?"

"No, you don't."

"I do."

Jennifer cursed under her breath and sat up.

"I'm going to sleep on a gurney down in an aban-doned hall."

"No, no. I'll let you sleep." The bed shifted again and then the room filled with light. "Have a good sleep, Dr. Mills."

The door shut and Jennifer lay back against the pillow. She didn't think she was going to fall asleep after her run-in with Dr. Rousseau, but once she closed her eyes again, sleep came easily.

The pager vibrated in her hand and she woke with a start. She flicked on the bedside lamp and saw it was coming from the ER.

It was her first twenty-four-hour shift, and even then she wouldn't go home after her shift was done. She had something to prove here and she would stay here as long as it took.

This was going to become her second home. Besides, her condo was sparse and empty. If she went home, there would be messages from her father. Invitations for her to go out campaigning with him, to show the voters she wasn't a pa-thetic loser like they all believed she was.

She just wanted to escape the stigma of it all.

She wasn't any of those things. She was a surgeon, for heaven's sake.

Only the more you listened to the naysayers, those creeping doubt weasels, the more you started to believe it.

And she hated that loss of control.

She hated that her confidence was all shot to heck.

Jennifer clipped her pager back to the waist of her scrubs and headed down to the ER. When she got there, it was relatively quiet.

"Who paged me?" she asked the charge nurse.

"Dr. Rousseau. He's in Room Three, needs a consult on a patient."

Jennifer groaned inwardly. "Thank you."

What patient had he dug up now?

Did this one have a tiger coming out of his chest? Tassels glued to the forehead? Cards embedded in the abdomen?

"Dr. Rousseau, you paged me?"

Nick glanced at her briefly. "Yes, the patient is adamant that they're seen by the head of trauma."

Jennifer approached the bed and then froze when she saw her father was on the gurney. "Dad, what happened?"

"Ah, there she is." Her father grinned. "I had a fainting spell during a speech at the convention center and they brought me here. Or rather I asked them to bring me here. I said I would be in good hands with my daughter."

Nick's eyebrows rose.

Jennifer pinched the bridge of her nose. "Dad, that's all well and good, but as I've told you before on numerous occasions, I can't assess you."

Her father looked shocked. "Why not?"

"Because you're my father. I can't treat family." She sighed. "You're in good hands with Dr. Rousseau."

Her father looked confused. "Why can't you do it?"

"I don't have time for this, Dad." She turned to Nick. "Please keep me informed, Dr. Rousseau."

"Will do, Dr. Mills."

Jennifer turned and left the trauma exam room, but Dr. Rousseau was close on her heels.

"Can I speak to you for a moment?"

Jennifer paused and crossed her arms. "Sure."

"I'm sorry I paged you. He was making such a fuss. I thought discretion would be the best bet. There's lots of reporters out there."

Jennifer's stomach clenched. The press. She hated the press. The damage they did, looking for sensationalist stories, but then again she was biased.

"It's okay, Dr. Rousseau."

Nick cocked his head to the side. "I don't think it is."

"No, it really is. Just…just don't spread it around that my father's here."

"Okay. I'll keep it to myself."

"Thank you. He doesn't need any more attention drawn to his campaign." She turned to walk away and then stopped. "When is your shift over?"

Nick grinned, his hazel eyes twinkling. "Are you asking me out?"

She blushed. "No. I just wanted to implement some changes to the schedule."

"Oh." She noticed he looked a bit disappointed, but then he shrugged. "As soon as I take care of your father, I'll be going home. I won't be in for another shift until Wednesday."

Jennifer nodded. "Thank you."

Nick nodded curtly and headed back to the exam room.

CHAPTER THREE

"Drag races? You dragged me to a drag race in the middle of the desert?" Jennifer shook her head as her best friend Ginny grinned and handed her a bottle of water. "We could've stayed at brunch in the air-conditioned bistro or gone shopping."

She needed groceries desperately and her condo was full of boxes. She'd been working for a week and still hadn't had time to sort through her stuff or make her condo a home.

"Chillax. This is fun!"

Jennifer rolled her eyes. "Yeah, because this is how I wanted to spend my day off, sitting on a hard bench watching motorcycles race across the desert."

"Yeah, but look how hot those guys are."

Yeah, she remembered that. Clearly.

Jennifer chuckled and couldn't disagree with her friend. Not that she could see any of the riders' faces. They had nice bodies clad in leather, and she was always a sucker for motorcycles.

Nick rides a motorcycle.

Her heart beat a bit faster as she thought about that moment she'd thrown caution to the wind and climbed on the back of Nick's bike. He had been a stranger, a man leaving on a long tour of duty, but she hadn't cared.

That had been when she'd still been carefree. Before the press had got hold of her and David had publicly humiliated her. Though she was more annoyed by the stolen research than the jilting.

The lack of accreditation of her in his paper had made her look like a fool in front of her colleagues. It had been like they'd all known David would screw her over.

David had broken her heart, but she could never regain her research. All the countless hours she and David had spent together, working on repairing an aortic dissection by trying a surgical grafting procedure with artificial veins, and he hadn't credited her.

Now the surgical procedure was being deemed innovative and the grant money he'd got for a medical trial he'd received, well, he had it made in the shade.

Whereas right now she would kill for some shade. It was too damn hot in the desert. She'd spent too long up north in Boston.

Even though she was wearing a big straw hat, it wasn't protecting her from the hot sun.

Ginny was whistling as her boyfriend, Jacob, climbed on his bike. Ginny waved at him, blowing kisses.

"So, once his race is over, we can head for a nice air-conditioned bistro or something on the strip?" Jennifer asked, grinning.

Ginny laughed. "If he wins, he keeps going until he's eliminated."

"Or wins it all?" Jennifer offered.

Ginny tapped her nose. "You've got it. Seriously, though, Jenn, thanks for coming with me."

"Of course. I'm sorry for griping. Not used to the heat. The North made me too soft."

"I still don't know how you survived all those bitter cold winters."

"Layers. Lots of layers." Jennifer winked.

Ginny chuckled. "Oh, they're starting!"

Jennifer turned to the race track. Two motorcycles sat there, revving their engines as the lights flashed from red to green.

In a split second it went from revving engines to a cloud of dust as the bikes raced across the desert plain in less than a minute.

Jennifer couldn't keep up with the fast pace and the screams deafened her. When the dust finally settled, there were two bikes at the end of the track.

"He won!" Ginny leaped up. "Come on, let's go down there. I promised him a kiss if he won."

"And if he didn't?"

Ginny grinned. "You don't want to know."

Jennifer laughed and followed Ginny down off the bleachers toward the track. Jacob and his opponent were riding their bikes back slowly up the side to where all the other competitors were waiting.

As they approached Jacob, he was shaking hands with the biker he'd just trounced and Jennifer had a nagging suspicion that she knew him.

Ginny ran ahead and threw herself in Jacob's arms while Jennifer lingered behind. As Ginny gave Jacob his reward, the competitor turned and Jennifer groaned inwardly.

"Dr. Mills," Nick said in surprise, running his hands through his hair.

"Dr. Rousseau." Jennifer took her large hat off. "I didn't expect to see you here."

"I could say the same thing."

Jennifer looked at Ginny, but she was still involved with Jacob and she was stuck here with Nick.

"I didn't know you raced bikes on your free time." Jennifer played with the brim of her hat, picking at some loose thread.

"Yeah, it's something I do to unwind."

"This helps you unwind?"

Nick smiled. "You knew I rode a motorcycle."

"Yes, but I wasn't aware that you raced it."

Nick shrugged. "Like I said, it's something I do to unwind."

"Most people read a book."

"I'm not most people."

Jennifer chuckled. "Sorry you lost."

"It's no big deal. Not really a professional at this. Believe it or not, I have another job."

"Really?" They both laughed together.

Stop flirting. Stop flirting.

"Sorry for interrupting." Ginny had that goofy

grin on her face like she always did when she was being mischievous. "Jennifer, I'm going to stay with Jacob in the tent. He can give me a ride home and you can take my car if you want to leave."

"I can take her home," Nick said.

Ginny grinned again. "You two know each other?"

Jennifer groaned inwardly. "We work together. Dr. Rousseau is a surgeon at All Saints and works in Trauma with me."

"She's my boss." Nick winked.

Jennifer sighed. *Great.* At least Ginny didn't work at the hospital. At least that rumor wasn't going to be started. Nick hadn't told anyone else about treating her father for heatstroke and dehydration.

No one was any the wiser and Mills was a common name.

"Sorry, Dr. Mills, would you like a ride home?"

"Not on your bike. Not today."

"You've been on my bike before."

Ginny's head whipped round. "You have? This is news."

Jennifer glared at Nick. "It was nothing. It was

a long time ago, so you can wipe that smirk off your face."

Ginny threw up her arms. "Fine, fine. So, are you going to take Dr. Rousseau up on his offer, or do you need my keys?"

Before Jennifer could answer, Nick stepped between them. "I'll take her home."

"Well, that answers that. I'll call you later, Jenn."

Before Jennifer could stop Ginny from leaving, she took off and Jennifer was left alone with Nick. Again.

It had been a bit of a godsend that he'd been off duty for a couple of days and the day he'd returned, Wednesday, had been her day off.

She'd managed to avoid him at the hospital. It had become easier to forget about him. To not think about him, but now, standing here in the middle of the desert, beside his bike, well, this was exactly where she didn't want to be. This situation was absolutely and utterly dangerous.

"Maybe I'll just catch a cab back home."

"Why?" he asked.

"Your panniers won't hold my hat." It was a

feeble excuse, but she was grasping at any straw to get out of this situation.

"I drove my car."

"Why? How are you going to get your bike home?"

"It isn't my bike. I don't have mine anymore." There was a hint of sadness in his voice. "I was racing a buddy's bike today."

There was really no escape.

"Okay. I would love a ride home."

Nick grinned. "See, now, was that so hard?"

She couldn't help but laugh then. "It was, actually."

"Let me just take the keys back to my buddy and we'll hit the road."

Jennifer nodded as he turned toward the competitors' tent. She watched him walk away from her. The dark leather molded his broad shoulders and the dark jeans were tight, giving her a good view of his butt.

He looked hot. Both in the sense that the heat of the desert was stifling and the fact she could picture her hands on his backside, squeezing the cheeks.

Don't look at it.

Jennifer turned away and watched as another drag race started and finished. She didn't know where Ginny had got to, but she was with Jacob. They'd spent the morning together. She knew she should head for home so she could get some unpacking done before she had to return to her duties tomorrow.

Nick returned, twirling a set of keys around his finger. "You ready to go?"

"Sure, if you are."

"I am. Won a couple races and lost." Nick shrugged. "It is what it is."

They walked in silence toward the parking lot, moving through the crowds. It was hard to talk over the roar of the motorcycle engines.

When they got to the parking lot, Nick stopped and pulled off his leather jacket. Underneath, he was wearing an indigo-colored V-neck shirt. The blue suited him, given the dark color of his hair, and she saw tattoos up and down his forearms, like sleeves. She hadn't known he had tattoos. They suited him, too.

He was such a stereotypical bad boy on the outside, but when he was in the hospital, he was so put together. So professional. Sure, he was a loner, that's what the nurses and other surgeons said, but he didn't look like the tattooed easy rider he was portraying now.

And she had a hard time thinking he had anger issues. He was so laid back.

He was an interesting character. So black and white, or was he? She had a feeling there was more to him.

"Whew, that's better. It was fine when I was out there on the bike, racing, but walking to the car, it's a little hot."

"Yeah, hanging out in the desert isn't my idea of a fun time," Jennifer said.

"What is your idea of a fun time?"

She grinned. "Air-conditioning."

Nick chuckled. "Come on, you were complaining about the cold temperature of Lake Tahoe. I believe you said something about people from the North having addled brains."

"What I said was that people up north are addled by the cold weather. I should know, I've spent the last several years in Boston."

"Boston?"

"Yes. I did my fellowship there."

"Yet I met you in Carson City."

"I was there to support my father."

"Ah, yes," Nick said. "The senator."

Jennifer groaned. "Don't remind me."

"Not a fan of politics?"

"No, not really. I mean I vote, it's just… It's a long story."

"I have time."

Jennifer shook her head. "I don't really want to talk about it today."

"Fair enough. Here's my ride." Nick unlocked the vehicle remotely. He drove an SUV. A black SUV, and it suited him, having been a soldier and everything. "Sorry, my car doesn't have air-conditioning, but we can get a nice breeze."

"It's great and it's exactly the kind of car I pegged you for. Though it's not really a car, is it?"

Nick opened the door for her. "You pictured me in an SUV? Are you stereotyping me?"

Jennifer slid in and he walked around and climbed in the driver's side. "No. I'm not."

"Sure you are." He winked at her and she rolled her eyes.

"Well, when you said you didn't ride a motorcycle anymore, the SUV seemed like a natural transition."

"Never really thought of that before." He started the engine and they pulled out of the parking lot, heading out to the highway. You could see the strip in the distance and in the rearview mirror were the mountains.

"I may complain about the heat and hanging out in the desert, but I do love this place." Jennifer sighed, letting her guard down.

"So why did you choose Boston?"

She shrugged. "Good surgical program."

"And you just decided to stay there?"

"You're asking a lot of personal questions."

Nick grinned and glanced at her quickly. "I'm just trying to figure you out. I like figuring people out."

"Why do I have to answer all these questions? Why can't I get some answers from you?"

"You haven't asked any questions."

Jennifer cocked an eyebrow. "Haven't I?"

"Nope."

"Okay," she said. "I have one. Why did you leave the army?"

Nick's demeanor changed in an instant. "I was honorably discharged. I didn't leave."

"Honorable discharge usually means that you weren't going to stay in after your tour of duty. Why did you leave?"

Nick's brow furrowed. "I was discharged. No big secret."

Only she didn't believe him. There was something going on there and she didn't know why he didn't want to talk about it. Then again, she didn't want discuss why she'd left Boston, why she hated the sight or any mention of David. Also, she was hiding the fact she was a senator's daughter from everyone.

As they approached the city, she saw a big billboard was up, plastered with a picture of her father asking for votes.

Jennifer groaned inwardly.

"So, why don't you want anyone knowing that you're the senator's daughter?"

"I told you, it's complicated and a long story."

Nick nodded. "Complicated I get, but people know."

"I know, but I like to pretend they don't. Helps me focus on my work."

"I get it, wanting to forget."

She was glad he didn't want to poke and prod any more. She wouldn't question him about his time in the army and he wouldn't bother her about her father.

"I don't want to go back into the city." She hadn't meant to say that out loud. It had just slipped out.

"Want to go to Lake Tahoe?"

Jennifer laughed. "No, that's, like, six hours away and I'm working tomorrow."

"Okay." Nick turned on his indicator and took an exit away from Las Vegas and the strip. They were heading east toward Arizona.

"Where are we going?" she asked.

"Hoover Dam."

Her eyes widened. "The Hoover Dam?"

"You sound nervous."

"I am! I hate heights."

He glanced at her. "Really?"

"Yeah, really."

"Oh, come on, it's wide and stable. We can walk around the top. You won't fall off. What do you say?"

"Okay, I guess. I've never seen it."

"Aren't you native to Nevada?"

Jennifer shrugged. "So? Have you seen all the touristy places in your home state?"

"No, I haven't."

"Where are you from? Am I allowed to ask that question or is that forbidden?"

"Illinois. I'm one of those people who have been addled by the cold weather."

Jennifer laughed. It was easy to laugh with him and she couldn't remember the last time she'd laughed like this.

She couldn't recall if she'd even laughed like this with David. They'd laughed, they'd shared good times, but she couldn't remember if it was the same. Which made her think it wasn't.

Which was sad, as she barely knew Nick.

What am I doing?

She was weak.

So weak.

Nick knew he shouldn't have offered to take her home and he definitely shouldn't be taking her to the Hoover Dam. At least, that's what he was telling himself over and over again in his head, but when he'd seen that it was her there at the drag races, he hadn't been able to help himself.

He'd gravitated toward her.

At first, all he'd seen had been a gorgeous, tall woman in plaid clam diggers, wedge sandals, a white eyelet blouse and a ridiculous straw hat. Her look was very rockabilly. So different from the classic Jackie O type of look she'd had going on when he'd first met her.

She intrigued him.

Still, he should've kept away. He should've walked away, and he was annoyed that now someone from work knew what he did in his spare time.

Only he couldn't keep away from her. He lost all control and he hated himself for it, but not totally, because now that he had her up here, he was glad he'd brought her.

Especially since she was standing in the middle of the Hoover Dam, her arms straight out on both sides, crouched over like the dam was actually rocking back and forth and she was going to plummet off the side.

It was hilarious.

"Shut up, shut up, shut up," she cussed at him. "It's not funny. I told you I was afraid of heights."

There was a definite hint of panic in her voice.

"I'm sorry." Only he wasn't. This was fun.

"I told you but, oh, no, you didn't listen to me."

He laughed. He couldn't help himself.

"I'm sorry, but if you could see yourself now."

Her eyes narrowed and she stuck out her tongue. She stood up a bit straighter and lowered her arms slightly, especially now that people were walking past and shooting her strange glances. One thing he'd figured out about Dr. Jennifer Mills was that she didn't like the limelight. She didn't like attention.

And he got it because being a senator's daughter probably didn't help.

Maybe that's why she'd become a surgeon. To hide away in an operating room rather than get involved in her father's politics.

Not that he blamed her for not following a career like politics. Politics bored the heck out of him.

Of course, he didn't know much. He'd followed his brother into medical school. He'd spent his whole life following Marc's lead, for the most part.

Except now.

Now he couldn't follow his brother's lead and the only set of wheels his brother was driving these days was a wheelchair, and it was his fault. His brother had followed him out there, to save him again, like he always had, only this time Marc had suffered for it.

When Nick had been discharged from the army, he'd decided to live differently. He'd sold his motorcycle, though it had killed him to do it.

It eased the guilt. At least, that's what he tried to tell himself, because really it didn't.

He'd settled into a good, respectable job instead of driving across the country and living in the back of an RV, experiencing North America.

When Marc had been injured, he'd sworn to himself he wouldn't be reckless anymore. Maybe if he showed his brother that he was trying to pull his life together, well, maybe then Marc would forgive him.

How can Marc forgive you if you can't forgive yourself? He shoved that unwelcome thought away, his fists tightening.

Get control. Control.

"There," Jennifer shouted. "I think I'm okay. I think."

Nick glanced over at her. Jennifer was standing ramrod straight, but at least she wasn't bracing herself not to topple over the side of the dam.

"Good, now why don't you come over to the edge and look out the viewfinder?" He wandered over to the viewfinder in question, expecting Jennifer to follow him, only she didn't. She stared at him like he had cats bursting from his ears.

"What?" he asked.

"You're crazy!"

Nick leaned over the edge, looking down at the Colorado River.

"Don't do that!" Jennifer shrieked.

"What?"

"You'll plummet to your death that way."

Nick chuckled. "Oh, come on."

Jennifer just shook her head. "No way."

Only he wasn't going to take no for an answer. He walked over to her and took her hand. "Come on. Where's your sense of adventure?"

"On solid ground."

He grinned. "First you didn't want to wade in

Lake Tahoe and now you don't want to come and see the splendor of the mighty, tamed Colorado River."

Jennifer rolled her eyes. "What's with you and bodies of water?"

"Come on. Indulge me and I'll never bother you again."

"Fine, but I'm holding you to that."

Nick laughed. "I'm sure you will."

He managed to get her over to the side, but her eyes were closed. Tight. Nick placed her hand on the side of the dam.

"See, you're safe. A high wall protects you. It's made of cement. Nothing is going to happen. Just open your eyes."

Jennifer let out a shaky breath and opened her eyes. "Oh. My. God."

He snorted. "It's fine. You're fine."

She took some deep breaths and glanced down. He watched her and couldn't help but smile. Being around her was like a breath of fresh air and the urge to kiss her again, to taste her lips, washed over him.

Nick clenched his fists and fought the urge to pull her into his arms. Like he fought every time he saw her, and every time it was getting harder not to give in.

She represented a moment in his life when he'd been carefree, when he'd been happy and sure of the direction of his life.

Nick cleared his throat and moved away from her. His hand was still on top of hers.

Get a grip on yourself.

"Well, why don't we head back to Las Vegas?" he asked, clearing his throat again.

"Sounds good. I've tested my fear of heights long enough." Jennifer moved away from the edge and quickly started walking toward the exit.

He smiled as he watched her, but then the smile disappeared when he realized again that he couldn't have a future with her.

Why did he always have to meet her when he couldn't have her? It was unfair but, then, life wasn't fair.

He couldn't have a future with her.

He didn't deserve a future with her.

Nick was unusually silent as they drove back to Las Vegas. It was a bit unsettling, because it was an awkward silence.

Jennifer hated awkward silences. They drove her batty.

"Knock, knock."

Nick shot her a questioning glance. "Are you telling me a knock-knock joke?"

"I'm trying."

He grinned. "You're trying? Do you have knock-knock joke learning disorder?"

"Well, they only work if the other party plays along," she said. "Now, knock-knock."

Nick shook his head. "I don't do knock-knock jokes."

"How can you not?"

He shrugged. "I just don't."

"Party pooper."

He sighed. "Okay, fine. I'll play along, but it had better be hilarious. I don't want to be let down by a mediocre knock-knock joke."

"Oh, the pressure is on."

"Do you fold under pressure?" he teased.

"Oh, no, I rise to the challenge."

He chuckled. "Fine. Lay it on me."

"Knock-knock."

"Who's there?" he asked petulantly.

"You're ruining it!" Jennifer screeched, punching him in the arm.

He gave her a strange look, like she was insane, and maybe she was. "How am I ruining it?"

"Let's try it again, shall we? Knock-knock."

"Who's there?" He batted his eyelashes.

"Better."

"Better who?"

Jennifer chuckled. "Sorry, I meant it was better."

Nick groaned. "Oh, please. This is why I don't participate in knock-knock jokes. You're making this painful!"

"Sorry. Let's take it from the top."

He groaned again. "No, let's not. This is the longest knock-knock joke ever!"

"I promise it's worth the wait." She smiled sweetly at him. "Please? I mean, I did go on top of the Hoover Dam for you. You can humor me."

"You're…" He trailed off, chuckling. "Fine, but this is the last time."

Jennifer grinned. She was enjoying herself; she liked torturing him. "Knock-knock."

"Who's there?"

"Howie."

"Howie who?"

"Howie gonna hide this dead body?"

There was silence.

"That was the most *pathetic* knock-knock joke I've ever heard," he said, mocking her before bursting out laughing.

Jennifer started laughing. "I know it's stupid, but you're laughing."

Nick shook his head. "I hate you a little bit right now."

"This is my street," Jennifer said. "Make a right."

Nick flicked on his blinker and turned into her quiet cul-du-sac where a row of townhomes stood at the edge of a new development. "Nice neighborhood."

"Thanks. It's quiet. Mine's the one on the end. Number twenty-four."

"Okay." Nick pulled up in front of her place and put his SUV in "park." The awkward silence descended between them again, only it wasn't so much awkward as something more.

Like the night they'd met.

It was heady and made her pulse race, her body heat. It made her feel nervous and excited.

It was dangerous.

"Thanks for the ride." Jennifer hoped her voice didn't shake.

"Hold on." Nick slipped out of the driver's side and ran around to open the door for her. No other man had done that for her.

"You didn't have to do that," she said.

"Any man of honor would." There was a twinkle in his eyes and he walked her toward her steps. "I had a good time today, Jennifer."

"Me, too." Her cheeks heated. They were so close, all she had to do was reach out and pull him closer. She wondered if he tasted the same or if she'd get the same rush if she kissed him.

Nick cleared his throat and stepped away, breaking the connection. "I'll see you around at work." He looked away and then glanced at her quickly. It was like he was fighting himself, his body and movements agitated. "Good night, Dr. Mills."

Jennifer watched him hurry away. She was disappointed, but angry at herself for letting it get that far.

They were colleagues. Nothing more.

Only for a moment she forgot all about that. She forgot about everything and it was nice.

"Good night, Dr. Rousseau," she whispered to herself as she watched him drive away toward the strip.

Even though she liked spending time with him, she just couldn't.

It was dangerous to get close to another man.

Especially the likes of Dr. Nick Rousseau.

CHAPTER FOUR

IT HAD BEEN two weeks since Jennifer had gone to the Hoover Dam with Nick. The night she'd almost kissed him.

She'd thought nothing of it, because they hadn't kissed. They'd parted on good terms. Or at least she'd thought they had until work. It was like Nick was avoiding her. At first, she'd thought she was seeing things when she would see him coming toward her and he would turn and walk in the opposite direction.

When it had first happened, she'd explained it all away, but for two weeks she'd barely seen Nick, who was one of her surgeons. She was head of trauma and one of her surgeons was avoiding her, and it damn well annoyed her.

And she knew people were talking about it.

There was something up and it was undermining her precarious authority. Which she'd been trying to build since her arrival.

She had yet to earn the respect of all her trauma surgeons.

Jennifer needed that respect if she was going to do her job well, and she *was* going to do her job well. She had something to prove, and even though all those who pitied her, who looked down on her, were over a thousand miles away in Boston, she didn't care because she'd sworn she would never be pitied again.

"Where is Dr. Rousseau?" she asked the charge nurse at the desk.

"He's in surgery. He's running a bowel for someone apprehended by the police. A suspected drug runner with balloons full of cocaine."

Jennifer winced. "How long has he been in surgery?"

The charge nurse looked at her watch. "He should be out soon."

"Can you have him come to my office when he's done?"

"Of course, Dr. Mills."

Jennifer nodded and headed toward the OR floor. It was then she ran smack into the man in question. He looked startled to see her and then glanced around, looking for an escape route. Only there wasn't one.

"Dr. Rousseau, I understand you were running a suspect's bowel for drug-filled balloons."

"Yes, I recovered three balloons and they are currently in the hands of police. The suspect is handcuffed in the recovery room and is expected to make a full recovery."

"Glad to hear it."

Nick nodded. "Is that everything, Dr. Mills?"

"No. It's not. I'd like to speak with you."

"About what?"

"About the trauma department and some procedures I want implemented. You see, I had a meeting about a week ago and you weren't in attendance."

"Someone had to be on the trauma floor."

Jennifer nodded. "I understand, but now you have to be informed and kept up to date. After you give your report to the police, come and see me in my office."

She turned on her heel and walked away from him, not giving him the chance to argue with her or make an excuse to get out of it.

He was beside her in an instant, his arm slipping through hers and dragging her into a supply closet.

"What're you doing?" she asked, or rather demanded.

Nick locked the door behind him, leaning against it. "Why do you really want to meet with me?"

"What are you talking about?"

"I was informed about the trauma changes last week when you sent out that memo."

"So, it doesn't mean I can't touch base with all my trauma attending on staff, does it?"

"It's because I've been avoiding you. Isn't it?"

Jennifer glared at him. "It has nothing to do with ignoring me. I'm trying to run an efficient and functional trauma department."

Nick took a step closer to her, his arms crossed. Suddenly she felt a bit like a deer caught in headlights. He was the oncoming car and she was stuck on the highway.

"I have a superpower. I can tell when someone is lying to me." He stepped closer again. "And you're lying."

"How am I lying?"

"You didn't really want to talk to me about the efficiency of the trauma department."

Jennifer stared him down. "Fine. I did want to talk about the fact you're avoiding me. We're trauma surgeons and I can almost guarantee you that we'll be working together again, so this avoidance thing, whatever it is, has to stop. I won't have this kind of behavior in my department. If you have a problem with me, tell me to my face."

He frowned. "Fine."

And that was all he said. She was expecting more, but there wasn't any more.

"Thank you, Dr. Rousseau." She moved past him to get out of the supply closet. She didn't really need to know why he was avoiding her, but at least it wouldn't happen anymore.

When she tried to open the door again, he stopped her.

"Dr. Rousseau, what are you doing?"

"I was avoiding you because…it's for the best."

Her heart skipped a beat. "For the best?"

"Yes, because when I'm around you, I'm fighting the urge to kiss you."

Her pulse began to race. "P-pardon?"

"You heard me." He moved closer to her and she retreated against the door, trying to keep her heart from beating out of her chest. She fought her own urge to reach out and kiss him, too. It was hard, especially since she knew what those kisses tasted like.

"Dr. Rousseau, I think—"

"We have to keep this professional, Dr. Mills. I know that. My avoiding you was childish, I know, but it's the only way I've been able to keep control."

"Okay, Dr. Rousseau, but we have to work together." Part of her was screaming to run. To turn and flee, but another part of her needed to know why he wanted to avoid her.

"Yes. I understand." Nick took a step back. "It won't happen again."

"Good."

This time she listened to her instincts and managed to get the door to the supply closet open and leave.

Nick watched Jennifer power walk away from the closet. She was running away from him. He was glad she was leaving.

He'd tried to keep his distance from her, but she was right—they worked together. They couldn't logically keep apart.

They had to work together.

Plus, she was technically his boss.

Which made her even more out of bounds.

Jennifer was trouble. Only she was the kind of trouble he craved desperately. The kind of trouble he missed.

Why the hell did trouble always follow him? Why was he so attracted to trouble?

Because it felt so damn good.

It had taken every ounce of his strength that night when he'd dropped her off not to kiss her. As they'd stood out in front of her place, there had been expectation in the air and he'd wanted to give in. He'd wanted to take her in his arms and drown himself in her.

Only he hadn't been able to.

His pager went off.

Damn.

Well, he didn't have any time to think about his own personal problems. Not now, with a massive trauma coming in.

He tossed his surgical gown and cap into the

soiled-laundry receptacle and grabbed a fresh scrub cap off the shelf before running off to Trauma.

When he got to the emergency department it was in absolute chaos. Jennifer was across the department in an isolation gown, directing traffic and clearing a path.

"What happened?" he asked a resident as he grabbed an isolation gown.

"There was a plane crash."

"A plane crash?"

"A private plane went down after a failed take-off." The resident turned and ran to meet the ambulances, and Nick was close on his heels.

Everything else was going to be put aside. Right now he was a trauma surgeon. Trauma was something he was good at.

Even after the stupid screwups he'd made in his past, all the reckless choices, he'd never failed in surgery. He loved what he did, and while he was in the operating theater, he forgot everything else.

He forgot his time overseas. He forgot the IED explosion. He forgot the look on his brother's face when Marc had told him that he was paralyzed, the look of blame on his face, the disappointment in his parents' voices. The guilt ate away at him.

Everything was gone when he was trying to save a life.

As the first patient came in off the ambulance, he let all of it go and focused on the patient. The rest of the world was just background noise. He could be anywhere and nothing would faze him.

It was how he'd survived on his tour of duty.

When the sound of war and chaos had been around him, he'd had to learn to drown it all out and focus on the soldier lying on the table in front of him. The brave man or woman who'd fought for their country and now needed him to save their life.

It was a survival instinct for him.

"Charge to fifty."

Nick looked up to see that Jennifer was working across from him. They were in the OR and he couldn't recall how they'd got here, but he was here now.

"Clear."

He moved his hands away as Jennifer shocked the heart, but the monitor still didn't move.

"Assystiline," the scrub nurse shouted.

"Charge the paddles again. Clear." Jennifer shocked the heart once more and the monitor began to show a heartbeat again.

"We have a sinus rhythm," the nurse said.

He looked at Jennifer across the patient. Their gazes locked, then they continued trying to repair the damage done to the man's spleen.

Nick hadn't had a chance to do a surgery with Jennifer, but the way they were working together almost seamlessly was something of a miracle. It was like they'd been working together for a long time.

"Dr. Murphy, hold the retractor, and can I have some more suction?" Nick cauterized and threw stitches as fast as he could.

"I think this spleen is beyond salvageable," Jennifer remarked. "I think we're going to have to do a splenectomy."

"Agreed."

Their eyes met across the table again. It was a moment that they understood each other, that they knew what needed to be done.

And together they would save this life.

* * *

"You did a good job in there, Dr. Rousseau." Jennifer scrubbed her hands.

"Why, thank you, Dr. Mills." Nick grinned at her.

"I've only had a chance to observe you from a distance; this was my first time working with you and I hope it won't be the last."

She watched his face, but he just nodded.

"I'm sure it won't be the last."

Jennifer rolled her shoulders. "I have got to get a coffee."

"I need to get some sleep."

"Sleep would be good, too."

Nick shook his hands. "I've been here for forty-eight hours. I need to crash like yesterday."

"Well, at least tomorrow you can sleep."

"Sure."

"Why, what're you going to do on your day off?"

"Drag racing. For my friend."

Jennifer grabbed a towel and dried her hands. "Why are you racing your friend's motorcycle?"

"He fractured his femur and can't, but he

makes the bulk of his livelihood from racing and I'm doing what I can for him."

"You miss it, don't you?"

Nick frowned. "What?"

"Well, you had a motorcycle with two helmets in the pannier. You seemed to love riding it, yet you gave it up, and I'm just trying to figure out why."

He shrugged. "Does it matter?"

"Yeah. Unlike you, I don't have superpowers."

She saw that half-smile again that made her feel a bit weak in the knees. It made her think of his body pressed against hers, his hand in her hair, holding her so close. He made her swoon.

"Well, I have nothing to hide."

"I think you do," she said. "We all have something to hide."

"Do you?" he asked.

If you only knew.

Only she didn't say anything and he was waiting for an answer. "No. Nothing to hide."

Liar.

He grinned, one that was a bit evil, and crossed his arms. "Nothing to hide, eh?"

"You know my only secret." She was a terrible liar. She always had been. "I'm a senator's daughter. That's it."

"And a former smoker." He winked and she groaned.

"Right. I forgot about that. I forgot you took my last cigarette and tossed it out into the bushes."

"I saved your life. Smoking is no good and you should know, you're a surgeon."

"Ha, ha, ha. I've been good. I haven't lit one up in a long time."

"Good." His hazel eyes were twinkling again. "Well, I'm going to get some sleep."

Jennifer nodded. "I'm going for that coffee. I still have another twelve hours and some paperwork I have to do before I can go home."

Nick nodded. "Good work today, Dr. Mills."

"You too, Dr. Rousseau."

CHAPTER FIVE

JENNIFER DECIDED TO have lunch outside in the courtyard off the cafeteria. She'd been stuck in the OR most of the morning and she needed a dose of vitamin D. Of course, the minute she stepped outside for a moment of peace, she ran smack-dab into Nick, who was sitting at a table under a tree and having some lunch.

Alone.

He had a book and a sandwich. All the other surgeons were sitting at tables, talking. Only Nick wasn't. He was alone.

There's a reason he wants to be alone.

She knew this. He didn't open up much.

Or perhaps the others had been avoiding him since that window incident, which was still whispered among the staff members when they talked about Dr. Rousseau.

She didn't know much about him. All she knew was that he was from Chicago, hated knock-

knock jokes and competed in drag races for his friend who had a broken femur.

Oh, and drove an SUV.

Just let him be. You don't need to get to know him.

That was what the rational side of her said.

The side that protected her from opening up to another man or another surgeon, because she'd sworn she'd never get involved with another co-worker again. It could only lead to heartache and betrayal.

Still, she couldn't help herself. She walked out into the courtyard with her own meager light lunch and gravitated toward him.

"I thought you didn't read?" she asked.

Nick smiled, but didn't look up. "Someone suggested reading as a way to unwind. So I'm doing that."

"Feeling stressed?" she asked cautiously.

"Not particularly," he said casually. "I just thought I'd give it a whirl."

"What're you reading?"

Nick glanced up at her, surprise etching his face, but only briefly, as he glanced down at his book. "*The Fellowship of the Ring* by Tolkien.

Thought it was about time I caught up on some of my old English assignments."

"A little late to turn them in now."

Nick grinned. "Yeah, but I figured why not."

"Do you mind if I join you?"

There was a brief moment she thought he was going to turn her away. Like he was searching for an excuse to say no to her in that pause that seemed to stretch for several agonizing minutes.

"Of course."

Jennifer sat down across from him on the picnic table, setting down her salad and her bottle of water.

"So, have you read Tolkien? Want to start a book club?" He waggled his eyebrows, teasing her.

"No, sorry, I can't say that I've had the pleasure of reading Tolkien. I tried once or twice, but I got distracted with other things."

Nick grinned. "Yeah, life has a habit of getting in the way sometimes." He put the book aside.

"So why do you eat out here?"

"Why not? It's beautiful out here. Nice shady spot, it's quiet and very conducive to reading."

"The nurses and some of the other surgeons tell me you're a bit of a lone wolf."

Nick snorted. "Really? A lone wolf. Is that all they're saying?"

"Yes."

"They told you about my temper and the window."

Jennifer fidgeted. "Do you want to talk about it?"

"What's there to say? I got angry at some pompous surgeon and took it out on a window instead of his face." Nick sighed. "I was fresh from the front. I haven't had an outburst since, if that's what you're worried about."

"I know. I've been told."

He nodded. "I really wish it had been his face. He was such a jerk."

Jennifer chuckled. "Well, it might've been best it was a window."

He grinned. "So you came out here because you feel bad for the poor old wolf?"

Jennifer chuckled. "Hey, I told you before, I'm just trying to figure you out."

"You seem so determined to categorize me.

Have you done the same for the other surgeons in the trauma department?"

"I have."

He crossed his arms. "Is that a fact?"

"I can read people, usually. Maybe it's the one thing I inherited from my politician father. He seems to be able to read people and get around them."

"Reading people is my superpower, too." He winked at her.

"I thought you said your superpower was telling if someone was lying."

He leaned over the table. "I have so many hidden depths. Besides, I thought you didn't have a superpower?"

Jennifer shrugged. "I lied. Guess your superpower failed you there."

Nick chuckled and she couldn't help but laugh with him.

"Seriously, though, why are you so antisocial? Are you afraid someone else will tick you off?"

"No, I'm just a private person. Besides, it's so noisy and chaotic in the ER that when I have a moment to myself, I like to have peace and quiet. A chance to decompress. When I was overseas there wasn't much opportunity to get a quiet moment. Working in a mobile hospital unit, you're constantly on the go."

"I bet," she said. "Where were you stationed?"

"Kandahar. I worked with surgeons from several countries, but mostly with the Canadian contingency that were running the hospital unit I was working with. My brother worked…" He trailed off and then cleared his throat, ending the conversation.

"You have a brother who's a soldier?"

"He was," Nick said quickly.

"I'm so sorry. Did he die in service?"

"No, he's not dead. He's in Chicago. Still practicing." There was a hint of sadness to his voice she couldn't quite understand, but she got the distinct feeling in the change of demeanor that the topic of his brother was completely off-limits at the moment and, even though she wanted to know why, she wasn't going to press it.

She was only his colleague. His boss.

That was it.

She didn't have the right to know.

She knew that, but she still wanted to know and that was a dangerous thing.

Get up and walk away.

"Well, I have to check on my patients." She stood up. "It was nice talking to you, Dr. Rousseau."

"Nick."

"Pardon?"

Nick smiled. "You can call me Nick. My friends call me Nick, remember? I think we agreed to be friends, or at least on friendlier terms."

Her heart skipped a beat.

"We're not friends, Dr. Rousseau. We're colleagues." She regretted the words, but they didn't seem to affect him at all. He was still smiling at her, that devastating one that had attracted her to him in the first place.

Dammit.

"Colleagues call each other by their first names. Besides, I don't understand why we can't be both."

"From what I hear, Dr. Rousseau, you don't have many, if any, colleagues who are friends."

"Ooh, harsh. Did you come over here today to insult me?" He winked.

It was annoying.

"Dr. Rousseau…"

"Nick."

Jennifer took a deep breath. "Fine. I'll call you Nick. Look, I'm just concerned about your loner attitude and the running of my trauma department."

He tilted his head to one side. "Is my lone-wolf status detrimental to my performance? Because I think you'll find that it isn't. The other day when we were working together in the OR, we worked seamlessly, and according to you, we aren't friends. We barely know each other. All we've shared is…"

"A kiss." Jennifer's cheeks flushed with blood and she gazed into his hazel eyes.

"Yes, a kiss. We've had intimacy."

She was well aware they'd had intimacy, and having that level of interaction with men never ended up good for her. She was a sucker for punishment, that's what she told herself as she sat back down.

"Why don't you have any friends?" she asked. It was blunt, but she had to change the subject, and fast.

Nick sighed and looked at her like she was crazy. "I have a friend. The guy I was racing for."

"I mean here at the hospital. Your place of employment. You've been here a year. I thought in the army you all were a tight-knit community."

"We were, and I can't tell you how many friends I've lost because of war. It makes me a bit wary to invest emotionally in someone I could lose."

"But you're not at war here."

Nick sighed. "It's a different kind of war I fight now."

Jennifer reached out and touched his hand, and his eyes widened in shock. Even she was surprised by it.

What are you doing?

She didn't know.

"Do you want to tell me about it?"

Nick pushed her hand away and stood, collecting the remainder of his lunch. "No. I don't."

"Why?"

"We're not friends, remember? You just said so yourself."

Jennifer sighed. "You're right. We're colleagues."

"Then what do you want from me, Jennifer?"

"No more avoiding me. If you have a problem with me, come speak to me, but don't avoid me."

"Fine," Nick said tersely.

Jennifer watched him walk away. She wanted to run after him, but she let him go. She didn't know what she was doing. Caring about Nick was not high on her priority list. Or at least she shouldn't let it be, it couldn't be. It wasn't her job. The only thing she had to worry about when it came to Nick was his ability as a trauma surgeon.

He may be a lone wolf, but he was a team player at least.

Jennifer didn't want the world knowing about her senator father or her ex-fiancé, so she got why Nick didn't want to share his experiences.

They say war changed a man, and even though she hadn't known Nick well enough before to determine if he'd changed or not, she could understand it if he had.

It wasn't her business to care. The only thing she had to concern herself with was his ability to practice medicine.

Only she did care.

She cared a lot.

* * *

Nick usually lingered around the hospital when his shift was over because really he had nothing to go home to. Work got him through the loneliness. Only, after his awkward lunch discussion with Jennifer, he had to get out of there when his shift ended three hours later.

He had to get away from her fast. When he was around her, he wanted to bare his soul. Let all the emotions he kept carefully bottled away pour out of him.

It was too easy to open up to her.

Only he couldn't let her in. If he let her in, then his guard would come down and he'd lose control. He'd become that careless and reckless person his brother believed him to be.

Nick had planned to return to Chicago when his time in the army was over.

Only plans changed. He'd taken his honorable discharge sooner than he'd ever intended and he couldn't go to Chicago. That's where Marc had gone and his brother had been adamant that he wanted nothing to do with Nick.

So Nick gave Marc his space.

He'd returned to Nevada, to the place where

a beautiful woman had granted him a boon and kissed him in the moonlight at Lake Tahoe.

Damn.

He didn't want a romantic entanglement. Especially with a coworker. He'd hurt enough people in his life, hadn't he?

He left the hospital, instead of working an extra shift, to avoid further temptation. He knew Jennifer was working there until at least seven and he just needed to get away. So he got into his SUV and headed over to Ty's garage. Maybe he could borrow the motorcycle for a while and just hit the open road. Let the world take care of itself and just forget about it all.

He parked in front of Ty's body shop. The garage door was open and Ty, cast and all, was sitting beside a sweet-looking black 1968 Ford Mustang GT-390. It had just been waxed and it shone as it caught the last few rays of the Las Vegas sun.

Nick whistled as he approached to let Ty know he was there so Ty wouldn't mess up the airbrushing detail he was currently doing.

"Sweet ride."

Ty looked up. "Hey, I didn't expect to see you today. Aren't you usually at the hospital?"

"I was," Nick said. "My shift is over."

"And you left the hospital on time? Dude, that's unbelievable."

"No, what's unbelievable is you're working with a broken femur. You're supposed to be on bed rest."

Ty snorted. "What're you, my doctor or something? Besides, I'm not standing. I'm sitting. I'm resting it."

Nick chuckled and pulled up a swivel stool to sit next to Ty. "Ha, ha. Very funny."

"I swear I'm getting rest, but I'm self-employed. I don't have the luxury of taking medical leave. It's bad enough I'm not out there racing and racking up business for my detailing."

"I get it. I'm sorry I can't race for you this weekend. Double shift."

"Nah, man. It's okay. You're a trauma surgeon. You have lives to save." Ty set down his airbrush and stretched. "So what can I do for you?"

"Wondering if I can borrow your bike for a ride?"

"Of course. You know where the keys are."

"Thanks." Nick stood and took the keys off the hook on the wall.

"So, you need to clear your head?" Ty asked.

"Yeah."

"Who is she?"

Nick tried to suppress his shock. "What?"

"It's a woman. It has to be. So, who is she?"

"Why does it *have* to be a woman?" Nick asked.

Ty chuckled to himself. "In my experience, it's *always* a woman."

Nick grinned. "Well, it's not."

Liar.

He knew his friend totally didn't believe him, but Ty wasn't one to pry. "Well, enjoy the ride. I can't tell you how I'm itching to go on a bike ride again."

"I hear you, but, seriously, get yourself back to bed or that leg will never heal. Do you know what kind of break it takes to fracture a femur?"

Ty rolled his eyes and flicked on his air compressor. "Yeah, yeah. Get out of here before I change my mind again."

"You'd better be in bed by the time I get back." Nick left Ty's garage and headed out back to where the motorcycle was waiting for him. It was calling to him. Riding the bike under a dusk sky on an open road into the desert was heaven.

He'd missed it when he'd been serving over-seas.

When he'd needed to clear his head over there, he'd learned to seek solitude instead of a ride, but it hadn't been the same.

The solitude felt good, but some real miles be-tween him and the ghosts of his past, or in this case Jennifer, was what he really needed.

He put on his helmet and threw his leg over the seat before popping the key in the ignition. The distinctive purr of the bike revving to life under him made him smile as he headed out of the city onto the highway.

When he was on the road he forgot everything.

Or at least he usually did, but not her. Not Jen-nifer. Instead, he was recalling every vivid detail of when Jennifer had ridden with him that one time. Her long, slender arms wrapped around his body, holding him close. Her breasts pressed against his back, her legs open.

Get a grip. You don't need an erection at this moment.

Nick turned the bike back toward Las Vegas. Back to the strip and back to the hospital.

He didn't exactly know what he was doing. All he knew was that he wasn't acting rationally at all. He had to see Jennifer.

When he pulled into his parking spot in the hospital lot, she was heading to her car. A briefcase in her hand and a coffee in the other. She didn't see him, he could leave. Only he couldn't.

"You know coffee late at night is not the best thing."

She turned and was visibly surprised to see him. "Dr. Rousseau, I thought you left at four?"

"It's Nick, remember?"

"My apologies, Nick. Aren't you supposed to be at home, sleeping?"

"I should be, after a night shift, but I'm wide awake. Must've been the coffee I had."

She smiled briefly, tucking her hair behind her ear. "Well, you've already clocked your maximum amount of overtime."

"I'm not here to work."

Don't. Do it.

She frowned. "Then why are you here?"

"I gave a lot of thought about what you said."

"What did I say?"

"About not having many friends at work. I don't let many people in."

She smirked. "You came all the way back here to tell me that I was right?"

"No."

"No, it's okay. I'm not complaining. I like being right." She grinned.

"I came back to see if you wanted to go have a drink?" That wiped the smirk off her face pretty fast.

It surprised him, too. Women and asking women on dates usually didn't make him feel so anxious.

"Right now?" she asked.

"No. How about in an hour? I'll meet you at the Petrossian Lounge at the Bellagio. Does that sound good?"

"More than good."

"So it's a date?"

"How about two hours? I would really like to shower after that nasty surgery I just got out of."

Nick laughed. "Do I want to know?"

"No, you don't." She smiled at him, her blue

eyes sparkling. "I'll meet you at the Petrossian at nine."

"Sounds good, Jennifer."

She blushed and walked swiftly to her car. Nick started up the bike, put on his helmet and headed back to Ty's to get his SUV so he could go home and shower.

What have I done?

Sealed his own doom, of that he was certain.

CHAPTER SIX

"YOU LOOK *GOOD*."

Jennifer bit her lip and turned to examine her butt in the full-length mirror again. She wasn't so sure about Ginny's assessment of her. It'd been a long time since she'd gone out with a man for the first time.

Even though she told herself over and over again that she had nothing to be worried about, that they were going out just as friends.

Did he actually say just as friends?

Jennifer *tsked* under her breath and ran her hands over her ivory lace cocktail dress, which was covered in sequins. It was the dress she'd bought on a whim a couple of months ago because it had been on sale and had had a designer label.

One that she'd kept trying to justify to herself over and over again.

See, now it's paying off.

"Would you stop fidgeting?" Ginny got up from where she was lying on Jennifer's bed and stood beside her. "You look hot."

Jennifer rolled her eyes. "Hot is not the look I'm going for."

Ginny grinned, in that mischievous, annoying way she had. "Why not?"

Jennifer couldn't help but crack a smile at Ginny. "Because he's a coworker."

"He's the guy from the drag races, isn't he?"

"Yes," Jennifer said.

"Come on, *he's* hot."

Jennifer just shook her head. "Hot isn't everything. Trust me. I know."

David had been good-looking. Devilishly good-looking. All the women at the hospital, even patients, had swooned over him. He was broody, powerful, confident and brilliant, and it was all an act. Jennifer had found out the hard way. The outer version of David was confident, but inside he was insecure and needy, and she'd been so blinded by love she'd given him everything he'd wanted.

She'd learned her lesson.

"It's just a drink between coworkers. That's it. Nothing more."

Ginny cocked an eyebrow. "Who are you trying to convince, because a casual drink between coworkers could happen at the local watering hole, but, no, he suggested taking you to the Petrossian during cocktail hour. That's something more."

Don't go.

A wave of sheer panic overtook her. Ginny was right. This was a date.

"I have to call it off." Jennifer turned around and made a grab for her phone, but Ginny was quicker, snatching it from her.

"No way."

"Ginny, give me the phone."

Ginny shook her head. "No way. You're not going to call and cancel. Even if this is more than just a drink between coworkers, which I *so* think it is, you're going to go and meet him."

"What nonsense are you spouting?"

"You've been working like a crazy woman since you arrived in Las Vegas. You barely go out and it was the same in Boston. I'm not an idiot. I know David hurt you, but you don't have to live like a nun, because he certainly didn't. Did he?"

Jennifer winced, reminded of how fast David had moved on when he'd left her rotting in her wedding dress, exposing her to the paparazzi who'd had a field day with it. They'd taken her down like a lion taking down a gazelle.

She'd gone into hiding until the heat had died down.

David had moved on with a vapid woman who praised him from the sidelines. Jennifer wasn't going to let her career slide to prop up someone else's.

At least, that's what she told herself when she'd donated the wedding dress to a secondhand store and focused on her career.

Of course, that left no time for anything else.

Or anybody else.

She stopped grabbing for the phone and Ginny grinned. "You know that I'm right."

"I hate it that you are." Jennifer sighed. "What am I doing?"

Ginny shrugged. "A date? Why are you so worried, does the hospital have a policy against staff members dating?"

"No, but I'm technically his boss. I'm head of the department."

And wouldn't the press have a field day with that.

Ginny shrugged. "So?"

They had a bit of a stare down and Jennifer sighed. "I won't call it off. It'll be fine."

"Of course it will be. Have fun. Let loose. You're so uptight and no one will be taking pictures of you. It's not going to be like that."

"Right."

Ginny handed her back the phone. "It'll be fine. Come on, I'll drive you to the Bellagio."

"Thanks," Jennifer said, hoping her voice didn't shake. Ginny left the room and Jennifer glanced at herself one more time in the mirror.

Even if this was a date, and she wasn't entirely convinced that it was, it was a one-time thing. Nothing bad was going to happen because she went out with Nick.

He was an unknown trauma surgeon.

Much like you.

And that was fine by her.

Ginny drove her to the front door of the Bellagio. A valet rushed forward and opened the door for her, and after the door was shut, Ginny powered down her window and leaned over.

"Hey, smile, and good luck."

Jennifer waved at her and took a deep breath as she headed into the Bellagio.

Why am I so nervous?

She'd been out with Nick before. Granted, it had been three years ago, so she had no reason to be so nervous, like the preteen wallflower she'd been in high school. When her father had only been Mayor of Carson City, and even though he had been well-to-do, Jennifer had still been socially awkward, klutzy and unpopular.

The woman at the front desk pointed her in the direction of the lounge.

You can do this.

Jennifer held her head up high and moved toward the bar. The casino floor was a hive of activity, but she moved through the crowds quickly and into the bar.

The sound of a piano drowned out the noise of the gamblers as she headed inside the elegant bar. A few heads turned when she walked past a group of well-dressed men, and that gave her the confidence she needed in that moment.

She smiled to herself and walked toward the other end of the bar, looking for Nick. She didn't know exactly what she was looking for; she supposed she was looking for the same leather-clad guy she was used to seeing, or the surgeon in the scrubs and the white lab coat.

When the designer-suited, dark-haired guy at the bar turned around, he almost took her breath away.

The sight of him in that impeccably tailored black suit was an assault on her senses. Her body suddenly didn't belong to her at that moment; it belonged to her hormones, which were sitting up and taking notice of the devilishly handsome man in front of her. He grinned at her and moved toward her. That damn smile that made her insides a bit gooey.

Get a grip on yourself. You're a surgeon. A respectable one.

And then she wondered what being a surgeon had to do with anything. Surgeons, contrary to popular belief, were humans, too, with needs, wants and desires.

She plastered on her best smile, but she probably resembled something akin to a frozen mannequin, her heart thundering in her ears and her stomach dragging at the bottom of her feet.

Don't forget to blink and breathe.

Jennifer suddenly felt like a real mannequin, badly posed and wooden.

Nick stopped in front of her and she let out the breath she'd obviously been holding, but wasn't aware until it escaped past her lips.

"Hey" was all he said.

"Hey" was all she could formulate in her brain at that moment.

"You look fantastic." Then he took her hand, brought it to his lips and pressed a light kiss against her knuckles. That simple touch caused a shiver of delight to run down her spine and her knees to shake, just slightly.

Jennifer pulled her hand away and cleared her throat. "An interesting choice for a couple of co-workers to have a drink, don't you think?"

Nick didn't respond, just smiled. "Let's find somewhere private to speak."

Her heart was hammering and she was worried it was going to burst out of her chest, but she followed him past the main bar to a small alcove, where a velvet couch was located.

She sat down on the low couch. They were completely hidden by a large white column, but she had a great view of the pianist on the grand piano.

"I'll get the first round—what would you like?" he asked.

"Um, surprise me."

"Really?"

"Should I be worried?"

He didn't answer, just winked and walked away. Jennifer leaned over to watch him walk, and as if he knew she was watching him, he glanced over his shoulder and smiled at her. A smoldering smile of promise.

I have got to get out of here.

Jennifer sat up straight and glanced around the bar. She'd never been to the Bellagio before; she'd seen it countless times but had never set foot inside.

The stained glass over the bar was beautiful, the piano music set the tone for a comfortable, elegant, but relaxed atmosphere. If she wasn't careful, she could get used to this. She could sink back into this couch and fall asleep.

"Don't doze off on me."

She glanced up to see Nick with two cocktails in his hands. He set the glass down in front of her. It was dark, almost red, with ice and a twist of lemon.

"What is it?" she asked, sniffing it. There was gin, definitely gin.

"A Negroni. Try it."

She took a sip and was pleasantly surprised by the oaky taste, which wasn't usually her thing, but this was good.

"Well?" Nick asked.

"I like it. What's in it? I taste gin."

"Vermouth rosso and Campari bitters." Nick leaned back. "Enjoy your drink before we head out."

She paused in mid-sip. "Head out?"

"We're not spending the whole evening in a bar, plus you look way too good to hide away here in the corner."

"Dr. Rousseau…"

"Nick." His gaze locked with hers and his hazel eyes had that twinkle again, like they had years before.

"Nick, you said to meet you for a drink. I'm doing that."

His gaze narrowed. "You're quite…unbending, aren't you?"

"Well, that's a nice way to put it. So I'll take it."

He chuckled. "Yeah, you can say that. I have to wonder why, though. You certainly weren't like this when we first met."

No. She hadn't been, and look where that had got her. David had flashed her a smile, several compliments and the next thing she knew, they'd been in bed together. She was much more reserved now.

Even with Nick, though their time together hadn't resulted in sex. It had just been a hot and heavy make-out session on the beach.

She'd been too careless in her youth.

"Good Lord, Jennifer. You're only thirty-four."

Jennifer tried not to snort as Ginny's voice infiltrated her thoughts.

"No, I guess I wasn't like that. I was a little bit more carefree, wasn't I?"

"A bit. As I recall, you were almost about to light up and then tossed your shoes over the fence you climbed to escape your father's event. Though at the time I didn't know that Senator Mills was your father."

"*Shh,*" she hushed him. "I don't want anyone to know."

Nick looked around. "You think there are paparazzi hanging around here?"

"There always seems to be, but they're like ninjas." Jennifer smiled. "A lot has changed in three years. A lot."

Nick nodded, his expression a bit more serious as his lips formed a thin line. "Yes. A lot has changed."

"You gave up your bike. That surprised me."

Nick shrugged. "Death trap."

Jennifer cocked her head to one side. "I find that hard to believe since you race your friend's."

He took a sip of his drink. "Like you said, things changed. It was no longer…feasible to keep it."

He was lying or hiding something, but then again she was hiding so much, too, so who was she to judge?

It was hard not to break down and confess his deep, dark secrets to her. Hell, it was torture not to pull that drink from her hand, pull her roughly into his arms and kiss her. Maybe more.

He'd known she was going to dress up, he just hadn't expected how utterly fantastic she'd look. Nick had known she'd look good, but he was so used to seeing her in business attire, scrubs or even a shift dress. Like the hot pink shift dress she'd worn the night they'd met.

He had not expected the ivory beaded dress that clung to her curves, and when she'd moved in front of him to sit down, he'd noticed the back was cut away, exposing an expanse of her glowing skin.

It was all he could do not to reach out and touch her just so he could feel the silky softness of her flesh.

He'd only planned to spend the evening in the bar, getting to know her or at least making an attempt so she wouldn't nag at him that he didn't have friends or try to. He hadn't been expecting this.

Nick's gaze was transfixed by her long, shapely legs as she crossed them, and the memory of their night on the beach flashed through his mind. Her lying out on the sand, their lips locked and his hand moving up her thigh, under her dress.

He cleared his throat and took a drink.

"So why did you sell the bike? Besides it being a 'death trap'?"

He laughed and swirled the liquid around his tumbler. "I had planned to be gone longer than three years. So I sold it rather than see it rot in a garage."

Liar.

He'd sold it and sent the money to Marc.

"You okay?" she asked, her voice gentle, full of concern.

"Of course. Why would you ask?"

"I don't know, you seemed to get so sad. Sorry if I brought up a touchy subject."

Nick smiled. "You didn't."

"So why didn't you stay over there? You said you planned to be gone longer. What happened?"

"An accident." Nick touched his face. "This scar is one of a couple I received when an IED exploded."

"Oh, my God. Well, I'm glad you're okay. Was anyone killed?"

"No," Nick said quickly. "No."

No, but his brother had been paralyzed and the man who'd been severely injured, the man he'd saved, had ended up taking his own life. He hadn't been able to live with the memories.

So his act of valor had all been for nothing.

Marc's injury. For nothing.

Just nothing.

"Well, that's a relief."

"Yeah, it is." There was a lump in Nick's throat and it was harder to breathe. He set his drink down. "Can we change the subject? I don't like to talk about my time over there."

"Sure," she said gently. "Of course. I don't mean to pry. I really don't."

"It's okay. Really, but I'd rather talk about something more upbeat, like this surgery you told me not to ask you about."

Jennifer groaned and laughed. "Really, you don't want to know about an abscess bursting during a bowel repair."

"Ugh."

"I warned you."

Nick chuckled. "That you did."

An awkward silence settled between them and Jennifer was fidgeting again, playing with wisps of her short blonde hair.

"So, where did you go after Lake Tahoe?" he asked, breaking the silence.

"Boston, remember? It's where I did my fellowship in trauma."

"Right. You did tell me. What hospital again?"

Now she looked uncomfortable. "Uh, Boston Mercy."

"Is that where Dr. David Morgan did his groundbreaking research?"

Something changed quickly in Jennifer's demeanor. Her expression became pinched and he knew he'd hit a nerve.

"Yes, as a matter of fact it is."

"Do you hold a grudge against Dr. Morgan or something?"

Her eyes flashed with annoyance. "Why would you ask that?"

"I've heard the gossip about you and Dr. Morgan."

Jennifer rolled her eyes, but then relaxed. "Yes, I worked with Dr. Morgan, but I don't want to talk about him."

Now Nick couldn't help but wonder why Dr. Morgan was off-limits for discussion. Had Dr. Morgan and Jennifer been involved?

That simple thought made him jealous and that flash of jealousy made him worried. *Who cares who she dated before?* Only he did.

Just the thought of that smug, smiling bastard on the front of that prestigious medical journal made him cringe inwardly, because he didn't want to think about anyone else's hands on Jennifer. Only his hands.

"Well, we seem to be getting off to a good start." Jennifer set down the empty glass. "All we seem to be able to discuss at any length is topics we don't want to talk about."

"Yeah, it seems that way."

End the night. You tried. It didn't work.

Only he didn't want to end it and that thought scared him.

"Do you want to go dancing?"

Her eyes widened in shock. "What?"

"Dancing? Do you want to go dancing?"

"You mean like to a nightclub?"

"Yes, but not one of those bass-infused places. I'm talking about somewhere classy, given how we're dressed, well, it might be a bit of a fast-moving place."

Jennifer looked unsure. So he held out his hand.

"Come on, Jennifer. Live a little, like you used to do before Boston's cold winters hardened your heart." He winked and she laughed, taking his hand. He helped her to her feet. She was slightly taller than him in those platform stilettos, but he didn't care.

"Lead the way, then."

"With pleasure. It's not far." Then he put his arm around her, his hand resting lightly on the small of her back, touching her soft skin as he ushered her out of the Petrossian toward The Bank nightclub in the Bellagio.

They crossed the busy casino floor out toward the north entrance, up the escalator to the night-club.

He paid the entrance fee and kept his arm around her as they entered the dark club, decked out in gold and glass. The place was swarming with glitterati and celebrities. Cameras were flashing like weird strobe lights.

Jennifer froze. "I have to leave."

"Why?" he asked.

"Photographers are all over this place." There was a hint of panic to her voice. How horrible it was not to have any privacy. He could hide at least.

"Just one dance with me. Besides, the photographers will be more concerned with the celebrities that are here. They're totally going to ignore two trauma surgeons dancing on their night off."

Jennifer smiled and nodded. "You're right." Though he wasn't convinced by her tone. It was like she didn't believe him.

Nick led her out onto the dance floor, which was a bit of a crush, and pulled her close to dance. His hands on her hips, her body moving with his.

What are you doing?

Yeah, he didn't know. He'd lost all sense and purpose. He couldn't think with having her so close.

Her lips were moist and red. The rest of the world was drowned out to him; all he saw was her. All he felt was her.

It scared him, but before he could stop himself, he leaned in and she sighed—not in annoyance or resignation but in anticipation as pink flushed her cheeks.

She wanted it, too, and, God help him, there was no going back.

"Oh, my God, Michael!" a woman screamed, shattering the moment. Nick looked around to see a young woman screeching, her companion passed out on the dance floor, his body twitching.

"Help! I think he's having a heart attack. Is there a doctor in the house?"

Jennifer and Nick glanced at each other.

"Me!" they shouted simultaneously and descended on the man on the dance floor.

CHAPTER SEVEN

"His RADIAL PULSE is weak." Jennifer shook her head. "Mr. Brannigan, can you hear me?"

The man just moaned.

"It might've been a CVA. Look at his face." Nick pointed to where the left side of the man's face was drooping. Mr. Brannigan looked to be no more than forty.

The music had ended and a lot of useless people were surrounding them. "Did anyone call an ambulance?" Jennifer snapped.

"Paramedics just pulled up at the north entrance," someone shouted.

"Thank God," Jennifer mumbled under her breath.

"We have to get him back to the hospital." Nick rolled the man on his side to make sure he wouldn't choke.

"The CVA could be caused by a clot, an aortic dissection… Anything could've thrown the clot." Jennifer glanced over her shoulder at the distressed woman. "Did he say anything before he collapsed?"

"Uh, no. I mean, he said he had some pain and then his speech slurred."

Nick frowned. It was then the paramedics showed up.

"Possible CVA. You need to start a large-bore IV and take him to All Saints."

The paramedic regarded him. "And you are?"

"Trauma surgeon at All Saints."

Working with the paramedics, they got Mr. Brannigan up on a gurney, out of the Bellagio and into the waiting ambulance.

Nick helped Jennifer up into the ambulance, much to the paramedic's chagrin. Then Mr. Brannigan's wife was in the back as well.

"Are you coming?" Jennifer asked Nick.

"I'll follow in my car."

The paramedic shrugged. "Might as well hop in, Doctor. It's all hands on deck."

Nick climbed into the back and the paramedic shut the door. Within a minute, the ambulance was racing along the strip to All Saints. It was a short ride.

The back of the ambulance opened and Jennifer was right beside the gurney with Nick as they wheeled it into the trauma department.

A nurse steered Mrs. Brannigan to the sidelines as Jennifer and Nick wheeled the patient into a waiting trauma pod.

"Could someone get my shoes from my office?" Jennifer shouted as she grabbed a disposable isolation gown from the wall, and gloves.

Nick had removed his suit jacket and placed it on the hook where he'd grabbed his gown from.

"I need to do a transesophageal echocardiogram. Make it happen and set up a CT scan, stat!" Jennifer shouted, sending residents and interns running in all directions. "I also need a neurology consult fast. Someone page the neurologist on call."

"What a way to end the evening."

Jennifer glanced up at Nick. He was grinning as he took the man's blood pressure.

"Yeah, it was." Jennifer moved to check Mr. Brannigan's radial pulses. "The left is weaker than the right. Could be a CVA or could be an aortic dissection. We won't know until we get him into CT."

"Well, let's get him down to CT." Nick turned to address an intern who was securing the IV pole on the patient. "Tell the neurologist that we'll meet him down in CT."

Jennifer cocked her eyebrows. "We? Is this a two-man job, Dr. Rousseau?"

Nick shrugged. "We hadn't quite finished our date, Dr. Mills."

She rolled her eyes and together they pushed the gurney out of the trauma pod. She kicked off her ridiculous stilettos when she saw the resident she'd sent off bring her sensible and comfortable slip-on sneakers.

Once she had them on, they pushed the gurney at a run to the elevator.

"Get out of the way!" Jennifer shouted. It was as she was pushing through the buzz of a bustling ER that a flash went off. Dread coursed down her spine and she looked back to see a photographer scurry through the ER. Though she wasn't a hundred percent sure that's what she saw. It could all be in her mind.

It's nothing.

And even if it was something, it didn't matter

at the moment. The only thing that mattered was saving the patient's life.

Everything else could wait.

It was morning when Jennifer, stilettos in hand, walked out of the hospital for a breath of fresh air. Mr. Brannigan's aorta had been dissecting and they'd discovered he had Ehlers-Danlos syndrome, a disease that affected the connective tissues. Mr. Brannigan suffered from frequent bruises and tears. High blood pressure from smoking had caused the lining in his aorta to weaken and dissect.

And since it was a type A and their cardiothoracic surgeon was busy doing a heart-transplant recovery, Jennifer and Nick had worked over Mr. Brannigan. Nick had done dissection repairs in the field, and before she'd chosen to work solely in trauma, she'd helped David on cardiothoracic patients. It was part of their research.

Mr. Brannigan was lucky that he'd had two trauma surgeons who knew what they were doing when it came to delicate aortic dissections.

Her shift started in an hour, but she was going to go home first and change. She didn't want her designer dress to get ruined or lost or crumpled up in her locker. As she stood there, she got some odd looks from patients.

She knew the sneakers and the designer dress didn't exactly go together, but her feet were a bit swollen from standing for so long, trying to save a man's life.

Nick stumbled out of the ER, stifling a yawn, his coat hooked over his shoulder. Dark stubble on his face, the sleeves of his white dress shirt rolled up to reveal the tattoos. They made quite a pair.

"Good job in there, Dr. Mills." He winked.

"You too, Dr. Rousseau." She sighed. "I'm going to head home to change into some comfortable clothes, maybe have a shower."

"Is that an invite?"

Jennifer gasped and then laughed. "You are bold, sir."

An older woman shuffled passed them, giving them a strange look, and Nick just chuckled.

"What's so funny? I've been getting strange looks since I stepped outside."

"They probably think you're a high-class call

girl." Nick waggled his eyebrows and Jennifer couldn't help but laugh.

"Are you serious?"

Nick shrugged. "This is Vegas after all."

Jennifer rolled her eyes. "How are you getting home?"

"I could ask the same thing of you. I can walk to the Bellagio, no problem. It's only a block from here. Is your car parked there?"

"No, my friend dropped me off. I'll probably call a cab."

Nick shook his head. "I'll drive you home. It's the proper way to end the date anyway. Come on." He held out his hand and, though she shouldn't have, she took it and they walked away from the hospital, down the street to the Bellagio.

Was she dreaming, because weird, surreal stuff like this didn't happen when she was awake. The only telltale sign was that her feet ached from standing in surgery for several hours. Add that to having a night out on the town after having just finished a shift at the hospital, she was surprised she was still standing.

They passed the Bellagio fountains up to the

main entrance, where Nick handed over his valet ticket.

"You paid for valet parking. Nice."

"It's easiest. Besides, I planned on impressing you after the nightclub when I took you back to my place to seduce you."

Heat flushed in her cheeks, until she realized he was grinning like a fool with a sparkle of devilment in his eyes. She punched him on the arm.

"You're a pain, you know that?"

Nick shrugged, not fazed. "So I've been told."

"Who told you that?" she asked.

"My parents, sister, old girlfriends and my bro…" He trailed off and his easy demeanor vanished.

"Your brother?"

"Yeah."

"You miss him, don't you?"

Nick nodded. "I do."

"So why don't you call him or go visit him?"

He shook his head. "It's not that easy. It's complicated."

"Ah, no need to say any more." She understood complications, living with her parents, watching her sister put up with an adulterous bastard all to save face. Her sister rarely talked to her anymore since Jennifer had pointed out that she should do something about Gregory and his lying ways.

Since then, she and her sister hadn't been on the best terms.

"You have a sister, don't you?" he asked.

"I do and we don't talk much, either, so like I said, I get it. She's a little miffed at me for suggesting her husband is a bit of a douche."

Nick grinned. "Is he? I mean, is that justified?"

"Oh, it's justified. He's cheated on her numerous times. My niece was born last year and he was at his mistress's house while my sister gave birth in the hospital on her own."

Nick frowned. "That's terrible. Gives the rest of the male population a bad name. Why doesn't she leave him?"

"That's the crux of our arguments. She's too afraid to leave him. She loves him and is blinded to his faults. She's not very confident."

"And you are?"

"I wouldn't put up with a cheat." *Again.* It was hard for Jennifer to judge anyone; it's why she wasn't angry at her sister. Jennifer knew that

David had had a couple of one-night stands, but still she'd stayed with him.

She'd been an idiot. She'd been in love, she'd been blinded by it, and David had taken advantage of that fact. Made excuses. Oh, yeah, she'd been in her sister's shoes. She was the last person to judge.

The valet pulled up in Nick's SUV. The valet opened the door for her and she climbed into the passenger seat.

Nick got behind the wheel and they drove away from the Bellagio.

"It's seven in the morning and the strip is still hopping," Nick remarked. "That's what I love about this city."

Jennifer shrugged. "It's a city. I prefer the country."

Nick raised a brow. "I find that funny."

"Why? My father was a rancher before he was a politician. He had this great ranch up in the foothills north of Carson City." Jennifer sighed. "Some of the best years of my childhood. There was no need for keeping up appearances."

"You needed to keep up appearances?"

Jennifer chuckled. "Oh, yes. I was a bit of a

rebel in my teenage years. It's where I picked up the nasty habit of smoking."

Nick nodded. "I was a bit of a rebel, too."

Jennifer leaned her head back against the seat and smiled at him. "So you said. Something about a pain in the ass."

"I didn't say pain in the ass. I said I've been told I was a pain." He winked at her.

"You're splitting hairs now."

He laughed, his smile so bright. She loved the dimples, even if they were covered by ebony-colored stubble.

She could so see the bad boy in him. The bike, the tattoos, the leather and the mystery he hid deep inside him. He may not admit to some deep, dark secret, but something was there and she wanted to find out what that was.

"So you were a bit of a rebel when you were a teenager."

"Oh, yeah. I was always getting into scrapes and Marc *always* bailed me out." He frowned, but only for a moment. "He always did warn me that one day he wouldn't be there."

"I'm sorry," she said.

"It is what it is."

"And how about now? Are you a bad boy now?"

He glanced at her briefly and grinned, his eyes dark with promise. "Would you like to find out?"

She blushed and cleared her throat. "Nick, you know that's not a good idea."

"Why not? We could always finish what we started on the beach three years ago."

"No, we couldn't." Though honestly she'd thought about that moment. Thought about how things might've been different if she'd allowed him to make love to her.

You couldn't change the past and she couldn't use hers as a crutch to keep her from the present and the future.

"Here's your place." Nick put the SUV into "park." "I guess I'll see you at the hospital in a couple of hours."

Jennifer nodded. "Yes, you will. No excuse. If I have to do it, you do, too."

Nick nodded. "Well, for what it's worth, before the aortic dissection and all, I had a good time with you."

"Me, too." It wasn't a lie. She had. It had been a long time since she'd allowed herself to let loose a bit. To get dressed up and go for a night out on the town.

"We'll have to do it again some time. Finish what we started, because I'm tired of having all these half-dates with you."

Her heart skipped a bit. She opened the door and slipped out. "Thanks for the ride home. I'll see you in a while."

She shut the door and jogged up the steps of her condo. Nick drove off and she watched him disappear around the bend, her pulse still racing as she toyed with the notion of going out with him again.

Why not?

For the first time in a long time, she couldn't come up with an excuse as to why not. There was a paper on her front step and the headline about a doctor caught her attention. She picked it up and the blood drained from her face.

Presidential hopeful's physician daughter moves on from famous former fiancé and parties with handsome ex-armed forces surgeon.

The paper was plastered with pictures of Nick and her at the Petrossian, The Bank and then running through the ER as they were working on Mr. Brannigan.

Jennifer swallowed the lump that had formed in her throat.

This was exactly what she didn't want. She didn't want this notoriety following her and, staring at the paper in her hand, all she could see was the picture of her running from the church, tears streaming down her face.

Senator Mills' daughter jilted!
Left at the altar. Senator Mills' daughter disgraced!
Dr. David Morgan: successful surgeon, breakthrough research and new woman in his life.
Dr. Mills' bitter heartache.

She couldn't go out with Nick again.
There was just no way.

CHAPTER EIGHT

SHE COULDN'T GET away from him now.

Nick had his sights set on Jennifer. She was in the scrub room alone, having just completed a surgery. He was going to get some answers.

She'd been avoiding him, and though that should be a relief to him—because if she was absent, he wasn't so tempted by the thought of being with her—it irked him to no end and he wanted to know why.

He barged into the scrub room. Jennifer jumped, then quickly glanced around her, looking for a way to escape. Only there wasn't one.

"Well, long time no see, Dr. Mills."

She regained her composure. "What're you talking about, Nick?"

"Oh, so it's still Nick, then?"

Jennifer frowned. "What has gotten into you?"

"Well, seeing how a couple of weeks ago you

were angry at me because I was avoiding you, I think the answer is pretty self-explanatory."

"I'm not avoiding you." She stepped on the bar under the sink and began to scrub her hands, vigorously. "I was in surgery."

Nick leaned against the doorjamb. "Oh, really? That's a long surgery."

"What're you talking about?" she asked.

"A surgery that lasted two weeks. Impressive. Do tell me about it."

Jennifer rolled her eyes and shook the excess water off her hands before grabbing a paper towel. "I've been busy. I haven't been avoiding you."

"I think you're lying."

Her eyes narrowed. "I'm not lying." She tried to push past him, but he put his arm across her escape route.

"I just want to know," he said. "Much like you pestered me when I was avoiding you."

"Ha!" She shot him a triumphant look. "Vindication. You were avoiding me."

"And you're avoiding me."

"I'm not, actually. I've been busy."

"Look, I saw the paper. I know you hate the limelight, but there's no reason to avoid me."

"Not avoiding. I am *head* of the trauma department."

"I get wanting to hide. Trust me."

"Do you want to talk about why you're hiding?" she asked.

"No."

"Well, then, now can you let me pass? You can't really hold me captive in a scrub room."

"Why not?" He grinned and leaned forward. "It's kind of exciting to have your attention like this."

Her eyes widened and she gave him the scariest stare; it looked a bit deranged as she moved closer to him.

"What're you doing?" Nick asked.

"I'm staring you down so you'll move," Jennifer said.

"It's freaky."

"It's not supposed to be freaky. It's intimidating."

Nick laughed. "It's anything but. The only way that stare is intimidating is because of its freakiness."

Jennifer stopped the stare. "I know Krav Maga."

Nick shook his head and stepped to the side as

she walked past him, but he fell into step beside her. He wasn't going to let her get off so easy.

She *tsked* under her breath when she saw him beside her. "Didn't my Krav Maga threat scare you off?"

"No, because, you see, I was in the army for quite a while. I know how to fend off Krav Maga."

"You're a pest." She tried to say it in a serious tone, but her voice broke with a chuckle. "Usually my threats with Krav Maga and the stare down work."

"You don't really know Krav Maga, do you?"

Jennifer chuckled. "You got me. Seriously, though, when do I have time?"

"So what happens when someone, for instance me, calls you on the Krav Maga?"

Jennifer stopped and turned to face him. "What do you mean?"

He grinned. "I mean show me your moves. Come on, show me how you'd scare away a would-be pest."

She smiled, her eyes twinkling, and held up her hands like she was trying to complete the crane move from *The Karate Kid*.

"Whoa, hold up there, Ralph Macchio. Don't be trying to sweep my leg or something."

Jennifer put her hands down. "Who? What are you talking about?"

"Have you never seen *The Karate Kid*?"

"No, I'm afraid I haven't. I grew up on a ranch and in my early childhood we didn't have television. No way to watch movies."

"We'll have to watch it together. Maybe you can pick up some more helpful moves in case someone else challenges you over your slick, nonexistent Krav Maga moves."

Then her easy, fun demeanor melted away. "Uh…sure."

Nick cursed under his breath. "Sorry, look, I just want to be friends." He was hoping that would smooth things over, but it didn't. Her cheeks flamed, as if that wasn't acceptable, either, and he became a bit frustrated. Women were so frustrating to him. Especially stubborn women like Jennifer. This was why he didn't get involved with women, yet she drew him in and it drove him crazy. He didn't know why, but it was a pain in the butt.

"I have to go, Nick." She turned to leave, but he

grabbed her arm and dragged her into the empty on-call room they'd stopped beside.

He moved in front of the door and flicked on the light.

"What're you doing?" she asked, her voice rising. "I have patients to see."

"No, you don't. I know for a fact you're coming off your shift."

"Are you stalking me?"

"No," he said. "I just want you to extend the same courtesy that I did. No avoiding. I thought we had a good time together a couple of weeks ago, yet something happened when I dropped you off the morning after. I don't know what and honestly I don't need to know, but no avoiding. I just want a peaceful work environment. I can't handle drama."

Her expression softened. "Fair enough. Friends, we can be friends." Though there was something in her tone that made him think that's not what she wanted, but it was how it was going to be and maybe that was for the best.

"Good." Nick opened the door and they walked out into the hall together. "I'm just starting a twelve-hour shift."

"I know. Who do you think made the schedule?" The mischievous twinkle was back in her eyes. He liked this version of her best.

It reminded him of the woman he'd left behind three years ago.

Before everything had got so messed up.

"I don't mind. You can give me a twenty-four-hour shift from time to time. I don't mind the long hours. Nothing else to do."

"No friends or family?" she asked.

"I think we've had this discussion before. Besides, I *tried* to go out once..."

"Say no more. I'll make note. I try to do long shifts on rotation to keep everyone fresh and on their feet. I've been taking the bulk of them, but I can certainly pass some on to you. I have things to do in my free time."

"Like making placards for your father's campaign?"

Jennifer laughed out loud. "Oh, he wishes. No, I keep out of politics and out of the spotlight as much as possible."

"Dr. Rousseau and Dr. Mills, I'm glad I found you."

Nick and Jennifer turned at the same time to see Dr. Ramsgate walking quickly toward them.

"Oh, Lord," Jennifer whispered under her breath, which made Nick chuckle.

"I'm so glad I found you both." Dr. Ramsgate stopped in front of them. "Most of my senior staff know, except you two, and I wanted to tell you in person. Dr. David Morgan from Boston Mercy is coming to All Saints for three months to present his research to our cardiothoracic doctors."

"That's good for the hospital. I read about his research in the medical journals." Nick glanced at Jennifer to gauge her reaction, but she'd gone quite pale. Her lips were pressed together in a thin line and her arms were wrapped around herself, like she was holding herself up.

"I'm sure you two will make sure Dr. Morgan feels welcome." Dr. Ramsgate glanced at Jennifer apprehensively.

"Of course," she said, but there was tension laced in her words.

Dr. Ramsgate grinned, obviously relieved but also completely oblivious. "He's hoping to get his hands dirty in the trauma department while he's here and possibly finding emergent candidates for his clinical trial."

"Of course," Jennifer said quickly. "If you'll excuse me, I have to get back to the trauma department."

Jennifer turned on her heel and ran away. Nick watched her flee, because that's what it was. He knew it had to do with Dr. Morgan.

"Is Dr. Mills quite all right?" Dr. Ramsgate asked. "I thought she'd be okay with it."

"I'm sure Dr. Mills is fine," Nick said, though he was lying through his teeth. He knew that. "She just got out of surgery. If you'll excuse me, Dr. Ramsgate, I have to get back to the trauma floor."

Even though he should probably leave Jennifer alone, he couldn't help himself. Something about Dr. Morgan irked her and he was going to find out what.

Only by the time he managed to get out of Dr. Ramsgate's clutches and head in the direction she'd disappeared, a large trauma was on its way in and Nick had to let it lie. Only he couldn't. She was hurting.

Who cares? You want to keep your distance from her.

Only he wasn't sure if he did.

Friends can care.

His conscience was right, but when it came to Jennifer, he couldn't quite help himself and that scared him.

He's coming. *He's actually coming here.*

Jennifer's stomach twisted in a sharp pang as what Dr. Ramsgate had said sank in. Again. She was nauseated and was trying very hard not to hurl, which ticked her off. She was angry at herself for allowing the memory of David to affect her.

She'd come here for a fresh start and she was better than this.

When did I become so weak?

Jennifer sank down on the cot in the on-call room. She knew the others knew. It's just she preferred it when they kept it to themselves.

And now that David was coming, that wasn't going to happen.

She cringed inwardly, thinking of the stares, the whispers.

The pity.

I need to go home.

Her shift had ended hours ago, but she didn't

want to go home. It was lonely there and she knew if she ended up there, she would think about David. Couldn't she escape the ghosts of her past?

Where did she have to run to? Alaska?

No more running.

That's what she'd told herself when she'd left Boston.

She'd held her head up high the best she could, but there was only so much she could take.

She had stuck it out as long as she could in Boston, but when David had won the Godwin award for all his research and then married that new woman, all within a year of breaking her heart, well, she'd run.

Run back home to escape the ghosts of her past, and those ghosts had found her.

"Oh, I didn't know… Jennifer, what're you still doing here?"

Jennifer glanced up to see Nick. He was in his scrubs and looked bone tired. "What time is it?"

"Three in the morning. I'm taking my first break. Trying to get some shut-eye before something else happens."

Damn.

"I didn't realize what time it was."

Nick shut the door to the on-call room. "I thought you left five hours ago when your shift ended."

"I meant to, but I…I lost track of time and I guess I dozed off."

Liar.

She hadn't realized she'd been sitting frozen in this position for so long. Which made her feel even that much more pathetic.

Since she'd come to Las Vegas, she'd had big plans to get her life back together. Sure, the presence of Nick had kind of thrown her for a loop, but it wasn't a big deal.

"I have to get out of here." She stood up and tried to push past Nick, but he grabbed her. "Let me go."

If he didn't, she was going to lose it. She was overtired, emotional. She couldn't cry in front of Nick. She couldn't.

If she did, she'd appear weak. She looked at him and couldn't help it, she couldn't keep the emotions bottled up.

"Jennifer," he whispered. "What's wrong?"

"Dr. Morgan was my fiancé. He broke my heart."

"I know." There was a hint of confusion in his voice. "Is that the only reason?"

Jennifer sighed and sat down on a cot. "I met him in the final year of my fellowship. Three years ago. After we…" She could feel the blush spreading up her cheeks.

Telling Nick about David felt like she was almost betraying him. Even though, after their night on the beach, which had been nothing more than a make-out session, there had been no commitment. Heck, she hadn't even known Nick's last name, but still the guilt gnawed at her. The embarrassment of admitting to Nick there had been someone else, and that was foolish.

"Go on," he urged. He hadn't even seemed to react to her admission about the two of them together.

"David and I worked at the hospital together." Jennifer sighed. "He was already an attending and I was a bit starstruck. He has a very big personality. It ended badly."

"Why did it end?"

Jennifer bit her lip. She didn't want to tell him

why it had ended. She didn't want to share her humiliation.

It was bad enough that it would be forever floating around in archives and internet caches. Anyone who wanted to do an internet search of her could find the headlines, the photos of her with a tear-streaked face, running from the church, and her father's pathetic speech saying that the family hadn't been disgraced by the unfortunate incident and that his party would still fund Dr. Morgan's research.

Most of all, she was worried Nick would think less of her for being weak. For being such a pathetic failure.

She glanced up at him. His hazel eyes were warm, full of concern, and she fought the urge to throw herself into his arms, to ask him to comfort her.

"Jennifer, you can tell me."

No. No, I can't.

Only she didn't verbalize the words, the words she fought so hard to say. She was very careful with her personal life.

And then the headline and the pictures of her and Nick racing that patient out of The Bank nightclub and photos of the two of them dancing, enjoying drinks and working in the ER flashed through her mind.

She couldn't have a private or personal life, thanks to her father and his presidential aspirations.

There was a page and Nick glanced at his phone. "Damn," he cursed under his breath.

"What is it?" Jennifer asked, thankful for the distraction.

"A major trauma coming in. ETA ten minutes. I have to get back to the ER."

"I'll come with you."

"You don't have to, you're supposed to be off duty."

Jennifer shook her head. "I'm here. I'm head of this department and I'm going to save lives. Let's go."

Nick nodded and they left the on-call room together, running side by side down the hallways toward the ER.

She'd managed to evade the answer to the question she didn't want to answer.

For now, but she was sure it wouldn't be the last of it.

And she knew she'd have to gird herself against the onslaught of press, against the presence of David working in her department again, because even though her flight instinct had taken over, she wasn't going to run from this particular ghost again.

She was going to hold her ground.

Which was easier said than done.

CHAPTER NINE

IT WAS A full day before the trauma from a multi-vehicle pileup had ended and Jennifer was flagging.

At least working on people, doing surgeries and saving lives drowned out her self-deprecating thoughts. She didn't think about David once.

She knew one thing: she needed to get home and get some rest. She could barely keep her eyes open since the adrenaline had worn off. It was so bad that not even coffee was working to keep her awake. She'd had enough espresso to give her the ability to see through time.

"You look beat."

Jennifer glanced at Nick. He was in his street clothes, a backpack slung over his shoulder. He was dressed like he was about to climb on his bike, clad in dark denim, leather and biker boots. He was such a contradiction. Inside the hospital he was smart and professional. Outside he was rough, rockabilly. He was the stereotypical bad boy. She almost expected him to pick up a guitar and get up on stage.

I'm really tired.

She scrubbed her hand over her face. "I'm exhausted, but also hungry. I've missed a few meals and a granola bar just doesn't cut it."

Nick nodded. "Well, you're in no state to drive. I'll take you out for a burger and fries."

Though she wanted to say no, her stomach growled happily in response. "Okay."

She propelled herself off the wall and followed him across the parking lot. She felt like she'd been scraped off the floor of a movie theatre. She felt sticky, gross and she didn't know what else.

Nick reached out and slipped his arm around her, effectively waking her up.

"What're you doing?"

He cocked an eyebrow. "Keeping you upright. You're lurching across the parking lot like some kind of drunkard."

Jennifer chuckled. "You're right. I'm exhausted."

"I'm not surprised." Nick opened the passenger side of his SUV. "Get in before you do damage to yourself or become a speed bump."

She laughed. "The way I'm feeling right now, I could *so* become a speed bump. I think that's a great profession."

Nick grinned, his eyes twinkling. He shut her door and then climbed into the driver's side. "I don't think you should take up the career of professional speed bump."

"Oh, why's that?"

Nick revved his engine and waggled his eyebrows before pulling out of the parking lot. "Such a waste of a beautiful woman."

Jennifer's cheeks flushed and she leaned her head against the side of the door. "So where are you taking me? It had better be a good place to get burgers. I'm a bit of a burger connoisseur."

"Is that a fact?"

"I love hamburgers, but I rarely indulge."

"There's a place on the outskirts of town, off the interstate west of here. It looks like a bit of a dive, but it's the best place I've found since moving here. I'm not a fan of burger chains."

"Me neither." Jennifer smiled at him. "It sounds great. I love little diners. Though if the burgers suck, I'm never, ever going to trust your judgment again."

He chuckled. "Deal."

She fought sleep, but it was hard when the rhythmic movement of the SUV was lulling her to sleep.

"Hey, sleepyhead." Nick shook her and she glanced up to see him leaning over her.

"How long have I been out?" she asked, hoping she hadn't been drooling or snoring. She'd been known to do that if she was overtired. Of course, that was according to Ginny and sometimes Ginny couldn't be trusted.

"About an hour."

She sat up straighter then. "You drove an hour out of town for a burger?"

Nick shrugged. "You told me it had to be good or you wouldn't trust my judgment again. I had to make this stop count."

Jennifer climbed out of the SUV. They were certainly in the middle of nowhere. To the east and west there were mountains, but they were on a flat plain of scrub brush and desert off a highway.

In the distance, she could see an outline of a town.

"Where the heck are we?" she asked.

"Are you complaining?" he asked, teasing her.

"No, just curious. This reminds me of home a bit, I mean with the mountains."

Nick smiled. "We're on the outskirts of Pahrump, Nevada and This Little Burger Shack has the best burger and fries I've ever had."

Jennifer saw the neon sign and indeed the place was called This Little Burger Shack and it was just that. A shack off the highway. It was not a restaurant, more like a double-wide trailer. People were ordering their food from a window and then sitting down under a metal awning to try and get some shade from the sun.

Although it was dusk and there was a chill in the air.

"Go grab us a table in the little bit of sun that's left and I'll order."

"How do you know what I want?" she teased.

"I think I know what *you* want." He turned and headed to the line, while Jennifer tried to hide the blush that was threatening to creep up into her cheeks.

She claimed the last table in the sun, but there was still a chill in the air coming down off the mountains. She reached into her bag and pulled out her dark blue fleece hoodie. It was ratty, but it was comfortable and she needed respite from the wind.

Being overtired and hungry certainly didn't help matters. She slipped on her hoodie and sat down on the top of the picnic table. The table had been painted neon yellow, but now the paint was chipped, and as she glanced down at the seat where her feet were resting, she saw there were initials carved into the wood. From the looks of it, some had been there for decades.

She couldn't help but wonder about those people.

Where were they now?

Those who had carved their initials in a heart with someone else's, were they still together? She secretly hoped so.

"Here you go." Nick set a cardboard box down beside her, which was overflowing with fries and one giant burger.

"I'm never going to eat all that."

"I just got a burger, we can share the fries." He sat down beside her, resting his feet on the seat.

He unwrapped his burger from its paper and

took a bite, chewing it and making exaggerated moaning sounds. "Heaven. I've missed these."

Jennifer shook her head and took a bite. It was good. Meaty, juicy and with a hint of garlic and something else. She loved garlic. "Holy, that's good."

Nick shot her an *I told you so* look and continued to eat.

They ate in silence, watching the cars traveling up and down Highway 160. The sun was setting behind them and to the east the first few stars were coming out in the blue sky. The moon was only a quarter full, which was good. It seemed to be on the full-moon nights that the ER would be packed with weird cases.

She crumpled up the wrapper of her burger. "That was good. You were right."

"I'm always right."

Jennifer snorted. "Sure. I hope I don't get food poisoning from eating a random burger on the side of a highway cooked in a trailer."

"I promise you, you won't. I missed having a good old-fashioned hamburger when I was overseas." He cleared his throat. "Anyway, glad you enjoyed it."

Nick changed the subject quickly, like he always did when he mentioned his time overseas. She knew she wasn't the only one with ghosts. Maybe that's another reason she was so drawn to him. She wanted to know what he was hiding from, but she also didn't want to push him. The last thing she needed was more drama in her life.

Right now she just wanted to enjoy this moment.

"I'm exhausted. I just need to get home and crash."

Nick nodded. "I'll take you home."

"Well, I certainly hope so," she teased, and he laughed. The uneasiness that had descended between them had melted away.

It was so easy with Nick, but also difficult because he was the type of guy she wanted to be with. She just wasn't sure she could open her heart again.

She wasn't sure if she was ready.

Or if she wanted to be.

Nick pulled up in front of Jennifer's place. They'd chatted for a bit on the hour's ride home, but then she'd dozed off again and he couldn't blame her. But when he pulled up in front of her place, she was absolutely dead to the world.

To be honest, he didn't try overly hard to wake her.

She looked so peaceful.

So instead he drove her to his place. He lived in a modular home at the north end of Las Vegas.

It was dark by the time he got home. He opened the door and made sure that Rufus, his black Labrador, was secure. Rufus was old; he just raised his head in question and wagged his tail politely. It was as if he knew that Nick wanted him to be quiet at the moment.

"Be right back, pal."

Rufus just let out a huff and went back to sleep.

Nick headed back out to the SUV, leaving the door to his home open, and reached in, picking up Jennifer in his arms. She huffed a bit, similar to Rufus, but didn't wake up.

He kicked the door shut with his foot. He'd come back later and get her bag and make sure it was locked.

He carried her inside.

Rufus looked up, wagging his tail, interested

in what Nick was bringing inside, but he didn't get up.

The door to his bedroom was open and that's where he took her. He laid her down gently in his bed and then tucked her in. He watched her for a moment, curled up on her side. So peaceful, so beautiful. He had to get out of there before he did something he'd regret, like getting into bed with her and taking her in his arms.

Only he couldn't move. He was frozen to the spot.

Why had he brought her here? He should've just woken her up and got her into her place.

He'd doomed himself. He reached out to touch her cheek, but she rolled over on her side and proceeded to snore. Nick pulled himself away.

He tried not to laugh as he backed out of the room, shutting the door. Rufus held his head up, cocking it to the side, listening to Jennifer's snores.

"Yeah, I know, pal. I had no idea, either."

Rufus wagged his tail, stood up and trotted toward him. Nick clipped on his leash to his collar and took him outside and then clipped the leash to the peg in his small yard so Rufus could sniff around and do his business.

Nick got his bag and Jennifer's out of the SUV and then waited until Rufus finished. His modular home sat up on a hill at the end of the community and from this vantage point, he could see the strip to the south.

He missed the stars.

The lights of the city drowned everything out.

The first time he'd seen stars had been when his dad had taken him and Marc out of the city. Out of Chicago to the Wisconsin Dells. They'd camped in a tent, their mother complaining bitterly, but it had been the stars that night which had drawn Nick in.

Brilliant.

The inky blackness had been filled with a million pinpricks of light. He'd stared at them until he'd fallen asleep.

I miss my family.

Chicago didn't offer the same view of the celestial heavens and he was learning that Las Vegas didn't, either. Too much light pollution.

Kandahar, however, offered the stars.

Often after a long shift, when there'd been a

lull in casualties, he would step out of the tent for a breath of fresh air and watch the skies, looking for falling stars. It had calmed him. It had been the only time during the blood, the wounded and the dead when he'd felt truly at peace.

Rufus let out a soft bark to let him know he was ready to go back in.

"Be right there, pal. Keep it down, though, we have a guest."

Rufus just pawed the ground and wagged his tail.

Nick dropped the bags inside on the kitchen table and then brought Rufus inside. Rufus trotted to his doggy bed on the floor, turned around three times and collapsed in a heap, letting out a huff as he settled for the night.

"Well, at least you're comfortable."

Nick glanced at his old rickety couch. He'd bought the home semi-furnished. It was a ridiculously large double-wide trailer with five bedrooms and a bunch of other rooms. It was a family home. He couldn't remember why he'd bought it other than he'd liked the location and it had been in his price range, but it meant that most of the rooms were empty, including all the bedrooms besides his. There was a kitchen and living room, which held the most uncomfortable couch on the planet and his television.

There was some work to do on this home. It had outdated décor and needed some things replaced. Nick had plans to flip it, but of course working at All Saints in the trauma department didn't leave him much time to work with his hands.

Nick ran a hand through his hair. He didn't relish curling up on the couch, which was too short for his length. He glanced at the bedroom where Jennifer was sleeping.

He could just curl up beside her.

Nothing was going to happen. His bed was a king-size bed. He could just keep on the other side of the bed and sleep comfortably.

He'd stay on top of the covers.

Don't do it.

Only his body told him differently. He headed straight for bed.

Jennifer was still curled up on her side, facing his bedroom window. Nick carefully kicked off his boots and pulled off his shirt and pants. He pulled on a pair of track pants instead of sleeping in his heavy denim.

Jennifer continued to snore.

He sank onto the far side, facing away from her. His body was quite aware that she was close, his blood heated and it took all of his willpower not reach out and wrap her up in his arms. He just wanted to keep her safe, but how could he keep her safe when he hadn't even been able to keep his brother out of the line of fire?

They were better off being friends.

Friends was safe.

Friends was easy.

Or so he kept trying to delude himself into believing.

CHAPTER TEN

JENNIFER DIDN'T KNOW what she was dreaming, but the most god-awful smell stirred her from her sleep, and as her body woke her up, she became aware of a panting sound. Really heavy breathing, which was mingled with the horrible breath.

She cracked open one eye and was met with a big wet maw, black with sharp teeth, a long, slobbery pink tongue and a wet nose.

"What the *hell*?" Jennifer shrieked, and jumped up to see a large black Lab sitting on the floor, staring at her with interest. At her shriek, the dog started barking. As she glanced around the room, she realized she wasn't at home.

The dog was a dead giveaway.

Jennifer calmed down and took stock. The dog was sitting on the floor, head to one side, totally interested in her.

"So, where the heck am I?" she asked the dog.

The dog panted and cocked its head the other way, as if to say, *I know where I am*.

"You're a big help."

The dog let out a friendly bark and then got up and trotted from the room.

She climbed down from the bed and cautiously headed to the door. The last thing she remembered was being in Nick's SUV and heading for home, so she assumed this was Nick's residence, but maybe not. Maybe he'd sold her off or slipped something in her burger. She wouldn't put it past him—he had, after all, given her a child who'd swallowed part of a birthday card for her first patient on her first day.

The absurdity of the thought made her chuckle.

She headed out into the main living area, which was open concept. There wasn't much furniture and there was no sign of Nick.

She caught sight of her bag on the kitchen table.

The dog who had given her her disgusting wake-up call was curled up on a ginormous dog bed and watching her with that forlorn look that most labs had.

"Don't look at me like that," Jennifer said. "Your master is a bit of a dingbat."

The dog wagged its tail.

She headed toward the bathroom. The door was partially open and she really needed to go. Maybe Nick was outside, getting the paper or something. She ran across the trailer and opened the bathroom door. She turned around quickly and ran smack dab into a wall of wet, muscular man flesh.

Blood heated her cheeks as she slowly looked up and saw she was currently pressed against a very naked Nick who had obviously just got out of the shower.

"Good morning to you, too." He grinned in that way that was hard for her to resist.

Run.

"Dang." Jennifer tried to disentangle herself but ended up hitting Nick in a spot she would rather not have. He doubled over and cursed in pain.

"Sorry!" she cried, as she fled the bathroom and tried to hold in her laughter. Her body was shaking from shock, embarrassment and humor.

Nick flung open the door. A towel was around his waist, but the rest of him was quite naked. His chest was hard and sculpted with muscles, including that V-cut muscle that made her knees feel a bit weak.

"Sorry to have given you a fright," he said calmly, but his eyes were still twinkling.

"You didn't, your dog did."

Nick glanced at the dog, which raised its head in question. "Rufus woke you up?"

Then it was a he. Well, that explained a lot.

"Yes, panting in my face. He has a charming aroma first thing."

Nick chuckled. "Sorry, he's quite venerable and doesn't usually get up to inspect guests."

A pang of jealousy shot through her. Guests? There had been other women here? "You often have guests in your bedroom?"

Nick grinned again, that devious one. "No." And that was all he said as he meandered over to the kitchen, opened the fridge and pulled out a carton of orange juice.

"Want some?" he offered.

"No, thanks." She ran her hands through her hair, which was standing up on end. A hazard of short hair.

"Suit yourself."

"Why am I here?" she asked.

"You fell asleep and I couldn't rouse you worth anything last night. So I brought you here to sleep it off." Nick poured himself a glass of orange juice. "Come on, nothing happened. You slept and snored most of the night."

Oh, God.

"I snored?"

"Like a lumberjack." He winked.

Jennifer groaned. "Sorry. I guess I took your bed. Where did you sleep?"

The question caught him off guard because he choked on the orange juice he was drinking and set it down.

"I don't like the sound of that." She crossed her arms and attempted the stare again. "Nick, where did you sleep?"

"With you."

"What?" She advanced on him and he held up his hands.

"No, it's not like that. There was nowhere else to sleep. I slept on top of the covers on the far side of the bed. Away from you."

"I ought to slug you." Then she sighed. "Well, thanks for taking care of me, but I should get home."

"Why?"

"What do you mean, why? Do you want me to spend the entire day with you or something? Haven't we seen enough of each other recently?"

"It's my day off and your day off. And tomorrow is a day off. Let's go for a drive." He smiled. "Come on, you know you want to."

She did. She really did. If there was one thing Jennifer loved, it was going for car rides, and she liked being with Nick.

Friends could go for car rides, right?

"Okay, you talked me into it. Can I at least use your shower?"

"Of course. There are towels in the top drawer of my dresser."

"I hope the door locks." She shot him a look, grabbed her bag from the kitchen table and headed into the safety of the bathroom.

Then she remembered she needed a towel. She opened the top drawer, which held socks, but there was a glint of metal and she pushed aside the socks to see a Medal of Honor resting there. Hidden.

Why was Nick hiding this? Most men would

proudly display their medals, but his was at the bottom of his sock drawer.

Maybe he doesn't have a place to put it?

Which could be a real possibility. Nick didn't have much.

"Did you find the towels?" Nick asked through the closed door.

"Uh, yeah." She closed his sock drawer and found a towel in another drawer. "Thanks!"

She shouldn't be digging through his things. That was his business. Just like certain things she kept from him.

Though she shouldn't spend the day with Nick, she didn't want to be alone.

Today she wanted to forget that David was walking back into her life.

Today she just wanted to be free of all that, even if only for a little while.

They'd been driving for some time and it wasn't until they got on Highway 6, which meandered through Death Valley National Park, that she realized they were headed to Lake Tahoe. Not that she minded in the least.

It was one of her favorite spots in the world and she hadn't been back there for a long time.

She was going to be exhausted the next day, but it didn't matter as she had tomorrow off, too.

"Why Lake Tahoe?" she asked, though she wasn't really complaining about it since she was enjoying the drive so much.

Nick shrugged. "Why not?"

"No reason. It's a great place, but isn't it a little far for a drive? I mean, who's going to take care of Rufus?"

"My neighbor's teenager. I pay him to do dog walking when I'm doing long shifts at the hospital. He is a dog walker for several dogs in the neighborhood."

"Oh, good, that's good to hear. I would hate to think that Rufus was locked up all day by himself."

"What kind of character do you take me for?"

They laughed together at that. "How long have you had Rufus? You said he was venerable."

"A year. He's a rescue dog. When I got back from Afghanistan, I found him in a Vegas shelter and I don't know…we were made for each other."

Her heart melted a little bit. She had a soft spot

for dogs, and especially for men who had dogs and treated them kindly.

Dammit.

"You've gone quiet. Are you a dog person, Jennifer?"

"Yes, of course. If I wasn't, I wouldn't have been as calm as I was with your dog's drooly mouth in my face this morning."

"Well, I promise to make it up to you, because I have a cabin at Lake Tahoe."

"How the heck did you afford that?"

"I have hidden depths. Though my cabin isn't much. It's basically a shack."

Jennifer chuckled. "You have a thing for shacks."

"Are you calling my home a shack?"

"No, but the burger joint and now this. Your home, from what I've seen of it, is nice. Empty, but nice."

Nick grinned. "Well, I spent all my money on my shack, so I couldn't really afford to furnish my sprawling modular home."

"I have one suggestion, though," she said.

"What's that?" he asked.

"Get another bed."

"You don't like sharing a bed with me?"

The blush was creeping up her neck again. She both loved and hated the way he affected her.

"You're not answering me," he teased. "You're evading my question."

"What was the question?" she asked, playing dumb.

"Sharing a bed with me and whether or not you liked it, which I personally think you did."

Jennifer snorted. "Is that a fact?"

"Oh, I know it is."

She laughed. "Well, since I don't really recall it, I can't comment otherwise."

Nick feigned horror, but she could tell it was all in jest. "To be honest, I don't really recall it either. I do remember having to put in some ear plugs so I could actually get some sleep."

Jennifer slugged him in the shoulder.

She couldn't remember the last time she'd felt so free, so alive. This was what it was supposed to be like with someone, and she couldn't ever recall joking and laughing like this with David. When she'd snored, he'd woken her up and sent her to another room, because he was a big cardiothoracic god of a surgeon who needed his rest.

In retrospect, she should've seen the signs a lot sooner, but she hadn't because she'd thought she'd been in love with David. Now she knew she hadn't been.

"You went quiet. Is everything okay?"

"Everything is fine."

And it was, for the moment, but she didn't know how long it could or would stay that way. She couldn't get involved with someone she worked with again—she couldn't because if something went wrong, she wasn't going to turn tail and run.

Only she could be with someone like Nick.

She'd always had a thing for bad boys and the only man she'd ever thought she'd loved, the man her parents had approved of, had been worse than any bad boy she'd gone out with.

The seven-hour drive flew by, surprisingly. They stopped to grab a bite to eat and take some pictures.

It was suppertime when they turned off the main road and headed down a densely forested laneway. Now she understood why Nick preferred an SUV, because there were so many ruts in the hard-packed dirt and gravel.

Soon they were at a clearing where a small A-frame cabin stood on the edge of a cliff that overlooked Lake Tahoe.

Nick parked out front. "Like I said, it's a shack and it's not on the beach, but I have a fantastic view. You can hike down to the lake from here, it's about twenty minutes."

"It's gorgeous." Jennifer climbed out of the passenger side and wandered over to the back of the A-frame.

"Actually, if you come inside, my deck has a nice view."

"Sure." Jennifer followed him in through the front door. The cabin was small. It was all open concept with a small kitchen and living-room combo. The back wall was entirely windows to enjoy the view and a large stone fireplace took up one side.

There was a mudroom with a washer and dryer and a bathroom on the other side of the entrance.

"Where do you sleep?"

"The loft."

Jennifer walked into the living room and looked up. Sure enough, there was a stairwell with a loft.

"From up there, you can see the lake. I also have skylights up there."

"More light?" she asked.

Nick shook his head. "I like sleeping under the stars."

Jennifer's heart skipped a beat at the thought of that and the night they'd lain on the beach together, under the moon and stars. She suddenly longed for that stolen moment again.

It had been before she'd had her heart broken. Before she'd been damaged and he'd been damaged by war.

They'd been so innocent back then.

"Want a glass of wine?" Nick asked, intruding on her thoughts.

"I'd love one."

"Head out on the deck and I'll bring you one."

Jennifer nodded and headed toward the wall of windows. There was a patio door and she slid it open, breathing in the fresh air of Lake Tahoe.

It'd been three years since she'd been back. She'd never brought David here. She'd kept meaning to and there had been plans to spend part of their honeymoon here. When things had ended, she'd been sad at first they'd never got to share this place together, but now she was glad that the memory of David hadn't tainted this place.

The only one she'd shared it with was Nick, and for that she was glad.

"Here you go." Nick walked out onto the deck, holding two filled wineglasses.

"Thank you, but you have to stop this."

"Stop what?"

"Choosing my drinks."

"What do you mean?" he asked.

"First the Negroni, now the wine."

He winked. "I can always take it back."

"I'm not complaining." She grinned and took the glass from him.

"And I haven't been wrong in any of my choices, have I?"

Jennifer shrugged. "That remains to be seen." She took a sip. It was a good wine and she wasn't a wine connoisseur by any means. Most of her history of alcohol involved long-necked bottles or lime and salt. She wasn't surprised it was a good wine. He did have an excellent taste in things, but she wasn't going to let him know that.

"Well?" he asked, leaning on the railing. "Was I right? It is a good choice?"

She leaned back against the railing beside him. "Yes, it's a good choice."

"Glad to hear it."

They gazed at the lake, with the sun setting behind the mountains. It was beautiful, as beautiful and calm as that night they'd first visited, and she wished they could stay here forever. Just like she wished that night, the first night they'd met, could've lasted forever.

"It looks like it'll be a clear night tonight," she said.

"Good," Nick said with a sigh. "It's why I bought this place, so I could see the stars."

"You like stargazing?"

"I do." He set his wineglass on the railing. "Growing up in Chicago, in the city, I didn't get to see the stars often. But after that, no matter what the strain or stress, the stars were a constant, they were peaceful and uncomplicated. It calmed me."

"Did it work when you were overseas?"

Nick nodded. "Always."

"Was it horrible over there?" she asked, though

she doubted she'd get a response. Every time she tried to get him to open up, he closed up again, building a wall back up, and she was no better.

"I know you don't like talking about it…"

"No, it's okay." Nick ran his hand through his hair. "Yeah, it was. It was war and war is horrible, but my job, my service to my country, that was why I joined the army."

Jennifer smiled. "You were passionate about being a medic?"

"I was." There was a bitter tone to his voice.

"Why did you leave?"

"I was discharged."

"So you've said, but from your tone I can tell it wasn't your choice."

"It was." Nick picked up his wineglass and finished the contents. Even though he'd said it had been his choice to leave, she didn't believe him.

"Why didn't you stay?"

"Why didn't you stay in Boston?" he asked, turning the question around on her.

"I told you."

"Ah, right, you were engaged to Dr. Morgan and he broke your heart."

Jennifer nodded. "Essentially."

"I think there's more."

She cocked an eyebrow. "You're turning the question around."

"How?"

"There's more to your story, as well."

Nick cleared his throat and straightened. "How about another glass?"

He reached out and tried to take her glass, but she pulled it back.

"My fiancé jilted me. He jilted me, and as a senator's daughter, I was publicly humiliated."

Nick's expression softened. "I'm sorry."

"Don't be sorry. I don't want pity. Pity was why I left Boston. Pity was why I ran." She was trembling, her hand was shaking so badly because she'd sworn to herself she would never let anyone else know what happened to her. She'd planned to hide, but she didn't want to hide from Nick.

Not here.

Not now.

"I don't pity you. I get why you ran. We all have ghosts we run from." He took her empty glass and set it down beside his.

"And what ghosts are you running from?" she asked.

He moved closer to her, making her heart race with anticipation. Nick reached out and touched her face, his thumb running across her cheek.

"I'm running from someone I hurt. Someone I cared for deeply, but who wants nothing to do with me anymore."

A surge of jealousy rose in her, thinking about Nick with another woman. "Oh, yes?"

"My brother Marc."

Thank. God.

"What happened to your brother?"

"He was injured in an IED explosion. Paralyzed."

"I'm so sorry, but I don't understand how it involves you."

Nick moved away from her. "My impulsiveness. I tried to be a hero and he got caught in the crossfire. We had a falling out. So, instead of returning home to Chicago, I came here."

"Your brother is in Chicago?"

Nick nodded. "Yeah, and I'm giving him his space."

Jennifer moved closer to him, placing her hand over his. "Nevada is a place you can get lost, I suppose, for both of us."

Nick's eyes darkened with something, a look

she'd seen before when they'd been standing in the lake. That look had taken her breath away three years ago and it was doing the same thing now. She turned away from him to get some space because if she stood here a moment longer, she wouldn't be able to control herself.

She wouldn't be able to stop what was coming.

Maybe I don't want to.

It was going against everything she'd promised herself when she'd come out to Nevada. She'd sworn she'd never get involved with someone she worked with again, but Nick was different. He wasn't like David. He would never humiliate her. Never hurt her.

How can you be so sure?

She wasn't, but right now she needed this.

"Jennifer, I'm so glad you came back to Nevada."

"Me, too." She bit her lip, her body thrumming with anticipation. His breath was hot on her neck, his lips so close she was sure he could feel her pulse racing as his fingers caressed her neck.

"Nick," she whispered.

He pulled away. "Do you want me to stop?"

Run. Save yourself.

"No. No, I don't want you to stop."

CHAPTER ELEVEN

NICK WASN'T SURE if he'd heard her correctly. They'd come so close to this moment, but each time it was interrupted, the connection broken and the magic lost. He almost wondered if he was asleep and dreaming this. If it was a dream, it was one hell of one.

She looked so beautiful standing in the sunset on his deck. The red and orange light of the sun setting made her skin glow, and when she smiled at him, truly smiled, it made his blood fire up and the need to possess her was too strong in him to fight.

Dr. Morgan had been an idiot to walk away from her, but he was glad he had, because if he hadn't, they wouldn't be here together in this moment. Again.

"Don't stop, Nick."

He pressed his forehead against hers, his body tensing as he held himself back from pressing against her. He wanted to take this slowly, he wanted to savor this moment so if it was merely a dream or a one-off moment in time, he could have it always. Relive it in his mind and cherish it.

"You're sure? I didn't ask you for a boon this time."

She sighed, her voice shaking as she reached out and ran her fingers through his hair, making his body tremble with desire. He wanted her so badly.

"I want this, Nick. I can't fight it anymore."

And that was all he needed to pull her tight and kiss her, drinking in the taste of her.

Vanilla. It was the same. He remembered these lips.

He'd dreamed about these lips for so long.

Jennifer relaxed in his arms, her mouth opening, and their kiss deepened. When they broke apart, he didn't let her go. He couldn't, as he stared at her, eyes sparkling and her lips swollen. He wanted to kiss her again.

"I think we should move this inside," she said, blushing slightly.

"What?"

Jennifer took his hand and led him inside and up the stairs to the loft. The only thing up there was his bed.

"We don't have to do this, Jennifer." Though he wanted to do it, badly.

Red stained her creamy-white cheeks, but only for a moment. "Yes, we do." And as if to drive her point home, she pulled her T-shirt over her head, kicked off her flip-flops and undid her jeans, pulling them down until she was standing there in a matching pink lace bra and panties set.

Even if he'd wanted to say no, he couldn't.

His pulse was pounding in his ears, his body singing with want and lust. She sauntered over to him, confident and sure of herself. So like the woman he'd first noticed, the woman he was attracted to.

The woman he wanted.

She wrapped her arms around his neck.

"Are you going to turn me down, or are we going to finish what we started?"

In reply, Nick scooped her up in his arms and carried her to the bed, pressing her against the mattress. This was what he'd pictured for so long, having Jennifer beneath him again. This time it wasn't the beach; she was in a bed. His bed, and there wasn't as much clothing separating them as there had been before.

He ran his hand over her body, trailing his fingers over her flesh, leaving a trail of goose bumps in their wake. It was too much to take in; his senses were overwhelmed.

"I want you, Jennifer. I've dreamed about this moment for so long, wondering what if." He pressed a kiss against her neck, making her tremble under his touch.

"Me, too, Nick. I want you so much."

He hesitated. He didn't know what he was waiting for, and maybe he was just trying to savor the moment. "I can't resist you and I tried so hard." His lips captured hers in a kiss, his tongue entwining with hers. Jennifer pulled him down onto the bed until he was on top of her. He took a deep breath, trying to regain control as she ran her hands over his body.

Reaching for him, she dragged him into another kiss. His hands slipped down her back, the heat of her skin driving him wild. He found the clasp of her bra and undid it painstakingly slowly, before he slid the straps off her shoulders.

The sharp intake of breath from her made his blood heat and when his gaze alighted on her state of half-undress, a zing of desire raced through his veins. He kissed her again, his hands moving to cup her breasts, kneading them. Jennifer closed her eyes and a moan escaped as he caressed her sensitive flesh.

She untucked his shirt from his pants before attacking the buttons and then peeling it off. It got tossed over her shoulder. She stroked his smooth, bare chest before letting her fingers trail down to the waistband of his jeans. He grabbed her wrists and held her there, before roughly pushing her down on the bed, pinning her as he leaned over her. He released her hands and pressed his body against hers, kissing her fervently, as though he would never be able to kiss her again. Even if this was just one moment between them, he was going to make sure Jennifer remembered it. She snaked her arms around his neck, letting his tongue plunder her mouth, his body coming alive as if it had been in a deep sleep.

He broke the kiss and removed her underwear, his fingers tracing over her calves. Each time his fingers skimmed her flesh, she let out a moan of pleasure, and when his thumbs slid under the sides of her panties to tug them down, she went up in flames. Now she was totally naked and vulnerable to him.

He moved his lips over the softness of her breast, laving her nipple with his hot tongue. She arched her back, wanting more.

"You want me, don't you?" Nick asked huskily.

"I do. So bad," she whispered.

His hand moved down her body, between her legs. He began to stroke her.

All Jennifer could think about was him replacing his hand with his mouth. The thought of where he was, what he was going to do made her moan. As if reading her mind, Nick ran his tongue over her body, kissing and nipping over her stomach and hips to where he'd just been caressing. His breath against her inner thigh made her smolder and when his tongue licked between the folds of her sex, she cried out.

Instinctively, she began to grind her hips upward; her fingers slid into his hair, holding him in place. She didn't want him to stop. Warmth spread through her body like she'd imbibed too much wine, her body taut as ecstasy enveloped her in a warm cocoon.

She was so close to the edge, but she didn't want to topple over. When she came she wanted him to be buried inside her.

Nick shifted position and the tip of his shaft pressed against her folds. She wanted him to take her, to be his and his alone.

Even if only for this stolen moment.

She'd never wanted someone so badly. She was driven by an insatiable need, one that only Nick could fill. Jennifer wanted him to chase away the ghosts of the past. Make her forget it all.

He thrust quickly, filling her completely. There was a small sputtering of pain, just like the first time. She clutched his shoulders as he held still, stretching her. He was buried so deep inside her.

"I'm sorry," he moaned, his eyes closed. "I've just pictured this moment a thousand times." He surged forward, bracing his weight on one arm, while his other hand held her hip. She met every one of his sure thrusts.

"A thousand times," he murmured again.

Nick moved harder, faster. A coil of heat unfurled deep within her and pleasure overtook her, the muscles of her sheath tightening around him as she came. Nick stiffened, spilling his seed.

He slipped out of her, falling beside her on the bed and collecting her up against him. She let him, and laid her head against his damp chest, listening to his rapid breathing.

What am I doing? What have I done?

She knew exactly what she'd done. Jennifer had broken the one cardinal rule she'd set out for herself since she'd left Boston and come to make a fresh start. She was angry at herself for being weak, but it felt so right. So good, and that scared her.

You don't have to be alone. You don't have to harden your heart.

It was time to move on. It was time to live her life, even if it was a scary prospect.

When she woke up, the sun was streaming through the skylights. She rolled over and Nick was lying on his back, a strategically placed pillow the only thing covering his body. His black hair was mussed and there was a thick growth of stubble on his face.

She grinned and moved closer. Now she could

see the tattoos closely. Not that she knew what the designs meant, or the roman numerals wrapped up in the intricate designs, but the tattoo sleeves suited him.

There weren't many physicians she was aware of who had them, but, then, they probably stemmed from his time in the army.

She ran her fingers through her hair and realized it was standing straight up on end. Moving as quietly as she could, she wrapped a sheet around her and tried to tiptoe to the bathroom, but her klutzy nature took over and she stubbed her toe against the end of the bed and let out a string of curses.

"Good morning," Nick said, before yawning. He sat up. "There's nothing like waking up to someone cussing like a sailor."

"Ha, ha. I stubbed my toe. I was trying to be discreet."

Nick grinned. "Well, at least I know I have you trapped up here. There's no running away and disappearing."

"I wasn't running away. I was going to the bathroom."

"What's with the sheet?"

She blushed and held her head up higher. "Discretion."

"You're a bit of a prude. I like that." He moved and tossed the pillow to the side, coming toward her across the bed.

Jennifer averted her eyes and took a step back. "You need to keep to your side of the bed, sir."

"Sir, now?" He grabbed hold of her sheet and tugged her forward. "I prefer Dr. Rousseau to sir."

"Stop! I'm trying to exit this room with dignity." Only she was trying so hard not to break out in a fit of giggles.

He stopped pulling. "Dignity? I've seen you naked." There was a twinkle in his eyes and he pulled her down on the bed again, pinning her down with his body.

"Nick, what're you doing? It's a seven-hour drive back to Las Vegas. We have work tomorrow."

Nick groaned and rolled off of her. "You're right. We do have to hit the road." He climbed out of bed and started pulling on his clothes.

"I'll go freshen up in the bathroom and then we'll head for home." She shot him a warning glance as she readjusted her sheet and headed down the stairs to the bathroom to make herself presentable.

When she'd managed to wash up the best she could in the very old-fashioned bathroom in Nick's cabin, she wrapped her sheet around her again and headed back to the loft. Nick was in the kitchen, washing the wineglasses and making coffee.

"That smells good," she said, her stomach rumbling.

Nick turned around. "It's just instant, I'm afraid. I haven't stocked the cupboard for the summer. There's a lot of work still to do. I don't have much time to do it."

Jennifer shrugged. "Instant is fine. We can pick up a muffin on the way back to Vegas. Provided it's not some random muffin from a shack."

Nick chuckled. "I swear. We'll hit a reputable chain."

Jennifer ran up the stairs and dressed quickly, in case she was ambushed again, and when she went downstairs, her cup of coffee was waiting for her on the counter.

Nick was outside on the deck. She was glad

last night had happened, though she'd sworn it never would, but at least now maybe she could work with him without all the sexual tension in the air. She didn't know where it was going or if anything would come from it, but at least sex was no longer hanging in the air. It was like a huge weight had been lifted from her shoulders.

She picked up her coffee and walked outside to join him. The air was crisp coming down off the mountains and there were some whitecaps on the aquamarine lake. She wished they could spend longer here, but it was a long drive back home. He looked over his shoulder as she approached.

"I didn't thank you for last night." She could feel the blush rising in her cheeks again, like she was some virginal young woman.

"You don't need to thank me," Nick said. "Last night was amazing, but what happens now?"

"Yeah, I was wondering the same thing."

Nick nodded, his face serious. "We can take it slowly. I know you came out of something bad and I…" He trailed off and she wondered what he'd been going to say, but she didn't want to press him. She didn't want to pry and ruin this moment.

"We can take it slowly." She wrapped her hand around the cup, savoring the warmth. "I don't want things to become weird between us and I do want to see where this goes."

"Yeah, me too. I can take it slowly. You're worth taking it slowly."

Her heart skipped a beat. "Thanks."

He smiled, making her heart melt a bit as he reached out and brushed his knuckles across her cheek. "No thanks needed for the truth."

"Truth. I'm hoping that we can tell each other the truth, that we don't hide anything from each other."

Nick's brow furrowed. "It's hard for me, but I'll try. For you I'll try."

"Good, and I will, too." She leaned over and kissed him, one that started as a peck and was quickly becoming something more. She pushed him away. "We have work tomorrow."

Nick grumbled. "You're right. Just promise me one thing."

"Of course."

"No more lame knock-knock jokes."

She laughed. "Finish your coffee so we can get out of here already."

"Okay, okay."

They finished their coffee, washed the cups and packed up the garbage, throwing it in the Dumpster at the end of the property, and headed back to Vegas. Only this time, they didn't take the scenic route, which was a shame, but it was after ten in the morning and they had to get back to Vegas in a decent time.

As they pulled out onto the interstate, Jennifer was bombarded every fifty miles or so with large billboards of her father and she groaned inwardly.

"Your father's campaign is starting to pick up," Nick remarked.

"I can see that. I was wondering why I've been getting a few calls from him."

"He's been calling you?"

"And I've been avoiding his calls. I don't have time to talk to him. Too busy at work."

Nick frowned. "Maybe it's not about the campaign. Maybe you should return one of his calls. I know if Marc called I'd answer."

"That's different."

Nick shrugged. "Not really. It's family."

"At least your brother doesn't want to use you

to win votes." At least that's how it felt when her father called her out of the blue. He'd never given two figs about her when she'd been mending her broken heart. He'd claimed to be busy with his work.

Now he was eyeing a bigger prize, he was calling her constantly.

She still couldn't believe he'd ended up coming to the hospital on her first day of work.

"Even if he did, I would take his call." There was a hint of sadness in Nick's voice and Jennifer felt guilty for griping about her family. They might be bothersome, but at least they were reaching out.

"How long has it been since you talked to him?"

"Too long. He got injured and had to end his tour of duty, whereas I finished out mine."

"I'm sorry."

Nick shrugged. "It is what it is. I just hope he finds happiness."

Jennifer sighed. "I'll call my father when we get back, but I promise you it's stuff about the campaign and I want nothing to do with that."

"Why?"

"The press. I don't want to be in the limelight, unless it's for my research." Her stomach twisted. "Only I don't have much time for research like I used to, working in Trauma."

"Yes, but I couldn't see myself working anywhere else." Nick shot her a sidelong glance. "It's a rush, saving lives when every second counts."

She smiled at him. His passion for his work was evident and she admired it. It was refreshing. To be a surgeon, you had to be all in and enjoy your job, but there was something deeper in Nick, the lone wolf of All Saints, and for the first time she really saw him.

And she hoped she could get back just an inkling of that passion again.

For so long she'd been moving like she was a zombie through a series of routines, hiding all her emotions, protecting herself so she wasn't vulnerable or exposed.

It made her nervous that he got to her that way.

For the rest of the journey they chatted about work and other things. It was an enjoyable drive. He talked about how he wanted to fix up his cabin and rent it out to skiers in the winter and rent it out in the summer when he wasn't going to use it.

He also mentioned he'd love to take a couple weeks off and just get lost in the wilds up there. Just him and Rufus. Jennifer was envious. She'd love to lose herself for a while. It'd been so long since she'd done that.

Tomorrow, when David showed up, she'd hold her head up high. She'd face him and deal with it. She had no reason to fear him, and being with Nick lessened the pain.

You don't need a man to prove your worth.

That was what her grandmother had always taught her and it was true.

So she'd face David tomorrow and show him she was strong. Show him she didn't mourn his loss one bit.

She was still the same surgeon she always had been.

CHAPTER TWELVE

JENNIFER STOOD IN the attendings' bathroom and checked on her makeup and outfit. The black pumps were killing her, but she wanted to look her best. She'd even put on pantyhose, which were bothering her.

Her white lab coat was starched and pressed.

She took a deep breath and blew it out and then made sure her red lipstick hadn't smudged her teeth.

You can do this.

The announcement was being made in the new trauma wing, which had still been under construction when she'd first arrived. The attendings from the trauma department would be there as Dr. Ramsgate unveiled it and introduced David to the team.

His research was about detecting dissecting aortic aneurysms before they dissected. The research she'd assisted on because she'd been in the ER and had seen them happen when they first came in and he was just the cardiothoracic surgeon who repaired them.

Don't think about it. Be gracious. The press will be there.

And that's what made her most nervous about this whole situation. The press. She just prayed that none of the press involved knew about her shared past with David. That it stayed in Boston, that all the questions today were about the new trauma wing and Dr. Morgan's work.

She opened the door to the bathroom and Nick was waiting in the lounge. He was wearing his white lab coat, but under that was tailored pants, a blue dress shirt and a royal-blue tie. He was clean-shaven and looked as starched and pressed as she was.

"What're you doing here?" she asked. "I thought you would've gone down with the other surgeons."

"You look beautiful," he said, looking at her from head to toe, which gave her a secret thrill.

"You're not answering my question."

Nick grinned. "I thought you'd want some moral support on the way down there."

"You're right." She ran her hands over her skirt again. "Ginny picked out my outfit."

"Ginny has good taste." Nick cleared his throat. "Everyone is waiting down there."

Jennifer nodded and took a deep breath, jamming her hands in the pockets of her lab coat. "Lots of press?"

Nick nodded and fell into step beside her as they left the attendings' lounge. "You're going to be okay."

"I have to be."

Nick nodded. "You can do this."

They didn't say anything else as they walked side by side to the new trauma department. When she walked over to the podium, there were some murmurs. Dr. Ramsgate, who had his back to her, turned when she entered the room, and as he turned she saw him. She saw David again and she felt like she was going to hurl.

He had a smug smile plastered across his face, one she wanted to wipe off with her fists.

Keep calm.

So she smiled, but one she was sure didn't reach her eyes, as she approached the podium. There were a few flashes as she approached and she had a sinking feeling that her story, her history with David, had preceded her.

I can do this.

"Ah, Dr. Mills, now that you're here, we can proceed. I'm sure you've met Dr. Morgan before." Dr. Ramsgate shifted to the side so that David could step forward.

The room went quiet as he moved toward her, his hand outstretched and that insidious grin on his face.

"Jennifer, it's so good to see you again."

"It's Dr. Mills, if you don't mind, and I'm glad you chose our fine facility for your *research*." It was hard to keep censure out of her tone, but David was unfazed and ignored it, like he usually did.

"Why don't you introduce me to your team?" David said, nodding at her six trauma attending standing in a row with their backs to the curtained wall.

"Of course, but I think we should get started. The press is getting restless."

David's eyes narrowed. "You would know all about the press, now, wouldn't you?"

She clenched her fist and counted to ten in her head.

Dr. Ramsgate got to the podium and welcomed the press. Jennifer stood next to David and tried to keep herself calm, like she was unaffected by his presence and didn't want to reach out and wring his neck.

She glanced over at Nick, who was standing at the far end, expressionless until their eyes met and then he gave her a quick smile and nod.

Jennifer returned them and then faced the crowd, trying to focus on the moment she'd unveil the new trauma wing with Dr. Ramsgate.

David leaned over. "I see you've moved on."

"You moved on as well." And she glanced at his hand. "Or is that over, too?"

David didn't answer her.

"And now our head of trauma, Dr. Jennifer Mills, will unveil our new state-of-the-art trauma facility that will serve the residents of Las Vegas and will save many, many lives."

There was applause and Jennifer walked past David and stood with Dr. Ramsgate. They pulled the cord together and the sheet dropped away to reveal glass, polished chrome and the beautiful fluid lines of a state-of-the-art trauma facility.

It took her breath away. It was beautiful.

She stepped in front of the doors, which opened with a hiss, and there was applause. "I would like to welcome everyone to All Saints Trauma. We have a dedicated team of surgeons, residents, interns and nurses to serve the greater Las Vegas area. One of our attendings would be happy to guide small groups through the department and explain the layout." She smiled as the press applauded and began to filter into the new trauma department.

Jennifer searched the crowd for Nick, but he'd been cornered by the press and was taking them through the facility.

"Impressive facility," David remarked, sidling closer to her.

"It is." Jennifer didn't want to engage in any social pleasantries, but he knew she didn't like to make a scene. He knew that she didn't like the limelight, which made his rejection of her all the worse, because he knew how to strike at her, to make it sting.

"You look lovely, by the way."

Jennifer didn't respond. She crossed her arms and stared at the trauma department, watching the press move through it.

"Oh, come on, you're not going to say anything to me? I'm here for at least a month minimum. You're not going to ignore me the entire time, are you?"

"Perhaps." She smiled to herself.

"Don't be so childish, Jennifer," David snapped.

"You don't want to start something with me here. You're goading me because the press is around."

David snorted. "Hardly."

"If you'll excuse me, Dr. Morgan, I have a tour to give." She left him, hopefully stewing in his own juices. She just didn't have time to put up with him, but at least now she knew she could handle him.

She wouldn't let him get inside her head.

She wouldn't let him control her ever again.

It took all of his strength not to go over and punch Dr. Morgan squarely in the face when he saw him all over Jennifer and Nick heard the comments he was making. Dr. Morgan was trying to bring her down. He was looking for power over her.

David was a bully. Plain and simple.

Nick detested bullies.

Maybe that's why he'd got into so many fights as a kid. Fights in which Marc had had to intervene and usually then they'd both come out of it bloodied, but they'd never lost.

Nick chuckled to himself at that thought and it dissipated some of the rage that was bubbling up inside him.

A month ago, he would've gone over to Dr. Morgan and clocked him one, or put his fist through another window. Something had changed, and the only thing it could be was Jennifer's presence in his life.

He didn't feel like such a ghost of his former self. For the first time in a while, he felt alive.

And he knew why, though he didn't deserve it.

He lost sight of Jennifer when he gave a couple of groups of press their tours around the trauma wing, but he was sure she was fine. She was a strong, capable woman.

So he made his excuse to Dr. Ramsgate and headed back to the old trauma wing, which would be shutting down tomorrow when the doors to the new wing opened up. Right now, he needed to be doing what he was here to do.

He'd been in the pit for a few hours when Jennifer came wandering in with signs notifying patients that the change to the new department would be at midnight. She was stopping and talking to people in the waiting area.

She may claim that she didn't want much to do with people or the limelight, but as Nick stood at the charge desk, doing his charts, he could see that people gravitated toward her. She had a way with people, and when she was in a room, their attention shifted.

He gravitated toward her. When she was around he couldn't help himself. Try as he might, he couldn't help himself.

And he didn't deserve her.

Yes. I do.

He'd taken it further than he'd intended to with Jennifer, and though he hadn't planned on it, he was happy that she was in his life.

He wanted to be with her and the thought of having happiness made him feel a bit guilty, when he had no reason to be.

He glanced back over his shoulder. She was taping up the signs on the doors, and as if she knew someone was looking at her, she turned and smiled at him.

Nick nodded and turned back to his charting, but soon the scent of her perfume tickled his senses and he knew she was standing behind him.

"Have the press left?" he asked, as she set extra signs down on the charge desk.

"Yes, for the most part. Dr. Morgan is eating up the spotlight."

Nick snickered. "He seems to enjoy the lime-light."

"That should've been a dead giveaway when we were together."

"Has Dispatch been informed that as of midnight they're to bring the ambulances around to the other side of the hospital?"

Jennifer nodded. "Yes. It should be a smooth transition. We'll leave everyone who is already in this trauma department here until they're discharged or moved off this floor. All newcomers will go to the new wing. Thanks for taking the midnight shift down here while I'm up there, making sure all the bugs are worked out in the new wing."

Nick shrugged. "I like this trauma department."

"You'll like the new one, too."

"Change for change's sake."

A phone rang and she pulled her cell phone out of her pocket and frowned. "It's my father. Again. I'd better take this or I won't get any peace."

"Do you think he saw the unveiling?"

"Oh, yes, he's probably wondering why he didn't get an invite."

Jennifer walked away and Nick let out a heavy sigh. He needed to distance himself from her, but he couldn't. She was like air. He needed her, only he was certain if he stayed with her he'd be her downfall. He'd ruin her like he'd ruined everything in his life.

CHAPTER THIRTEEN

"WELL, FINALLY YOU'VE decided to return one of my calls," her father said petulantly over the phone.

Jennifer rolled her eyes. "I've been busy. I'm a trauma surgeon, Dad. The ER can get a bit chaotic."

"I don't think you've been that busy." There was something in the tone of his voice that made her stomach sink and skin crawl. He knew about the trauma wing and he was angry she hadn't told him about it, but she hadn't wanted the opening of the new wing of the hospital to be overshadowed by her father's campaign.

Besides, she didn't want her father and David in the same room. Not after her father had taken David's side when she'd been jilted.

"Look, today was a small gathering of press and surgeons. I couldn't make room for your campaign to be there."

"What're you talking about?" he asked, thoroughly confused.

"The press conference today that was televised. The hospital opened a new trauma department." She deliberately glossed over the fact that David was there.

"Well…I can't say that I'm not disappointed you didn't include me or my campaign in that venture. You know how much I support hospitals and healthcare equality."

"I know, I know. I'm sorry, Dad. Next time." She crossed her fingers and hoped he didn't know she was lying through her teeth.

"That's not the publicity I'm calling about, Jennifer."

"What publicity are you calling about, then?"

He sighed. "Have you looked at today's paper?"

"No." It was harder to breathe and she ran into the attendings' lounge, which thankfully was devoid of any surgeons. She searched through the pile of papers on the coffee table and the moment she found it she dropped to her knees and tried not to faint.

"Oh, my God," she whispered.

"You see. It's all over the place and I know Dr.

Morgan is in Las Vegas. There's no denying it. This, coupled with this new *friend* of yours... Well, I think it's best to keep a low profile."

It was a warning—she didn't mistake his words or his tone.

"It doesn't matter who he is."

"Jennifer, the pictures show you spending a weekend with him, both in a trailer and a cabin at Lake Tahoe."

A headache began to form right behind her eyes. "I can see the pictures, Dad."

"Then you should know that you have to be more aware that the press is following you. You are a senator's daughter, a daughter of someone who is trying to become a candidate to run for president. You have to be more discreet."

"I have to go, Dad."

"Promise me this won't happen again."

"Goodbye, Dad." Jennifer hung up the phone, even though she could still hear him protesting on the line.

No matter what she did, she couldn't be discreet enough for her father's liking. What was she supposed to do, remain celibate? Never find love or happiness?

Yes. That's it exactly.

That's exactly what she'd set out to do and then she'd ended up in the same hospital as Nick. She glanced at the headlines.

Senator Mills' daughter's wild weekend with fellow surgeon.
Love nest at Lake Tahoe.

There was a picture of Nick carrying her into his home, but more horrifying was the blurry picture of the two of them in bed, in his cabin, the morning after. They'd followed them to Nick's property and invaded their privacy.

Nick was a private man.

He was going to be so mad when he saw the pictures, the headlines. He'd never want to see her again.

This is why I should've never gotten involved with someone at work.

She'd brought this on herself and she would face whatever came her way. Even if it meant that another man she loved walked out of her life.

Love? Did she love Nick?

The realization hit her like a ton of bricks. She

loved him. When they were together, it was so easy and she forgot about everything else.

I have to get out of here.

Only she couldn't escape quite yet. Her shift didn't end until after midnight. Right now, she had to get her head together and finish her work. She wasn't going to run away from the headlines, she wasn't going to run away from David and she certainly wasn't going to run away from Nick.

She picked herself up and slammed the paper back down on the table.

"You know, I caught the headlines this morning."

Jennifer spun around and saw David standing in the doorway, that smug smile on his face. How had she ever fallen for him? Sure, he was handsome, but now she could see how shallow he was. Hindsight was twenty-twenty and she couldn't change the past.

"I'm glad to hear you can read."

"You were always bad at jokes, Jennifer." He moved toward her, picking up the paper she'd discarded. "Isn't this the surgeon currently working on the old trauma floor?"

"Dr. Rousseau? Yes, it is, he's a friend of mine."

David raised his eyebrows. "Just a friend?"

Jennifer crossed her arms. "What's it to you?"

"Just looking out for your best interest. You know I care about you." And then he reached out, trying to touch her, but Jennifer stepped away.

"Don't touch me."

"Come on, Jenny. Can't I apologize for what I did to you? Can't we make up?"

"My name is Jennifer and you call this making up?" She shook her head.

"What're you talking about? I always called you Jenny."

"I didn't like it then and I don't like it now." She pushed past him, but he grabbed her arm and pulled her back. "Let go of me."

"I just want to talk," he snapped. "What's wrong with that?"

"Let go of me. This is your final warning!"

"Or you'll do what? Come on, Jenny, you don't—"

Jennifer stamped her heeled foot onto the top of his foot hard, making him curse in pain as he reached down to cradle his foot and his newly scuffed leather shoes.

She smiled at her handiwork before leaving the

attendings' lounge to get away from him. She wanted nothing to do with him.

Right now, she needed to get back to work. Everything else could wait until later.

There was a knock on her door at three in the morning. She should just ignore it, but it was incessant and she didn't want whoever it was to wake her neighbors. If it was David, she was going to do more than just step on his foot, she was going to take him by the... Well, she was going to hurt him.

The knocking started again as she peeked through the peephole. It was Nick, standing on her doorstep, in his leather jacket and holding the paper.

Jennifer groaned inwardly and opened the door.

"Hey," Nick said, but there was no hint of humor, no smile.

"What're you doing here?"

"Can I come in?"

Jennifer nodded and let him inside. She shut the door. "I see you saw the headlines."

Nick glanced at the paper in his hand. "What, this?"

"Yeah, that." Jennifer moved past him and toward the kitchen, and she heard him following her. She flicked on her kettle. "Want some coffee?"

"No, I think I'm going to turn it down. I just got off my shift and need to sleep."

Jennifer nodded. "Well, I'm not sleeping anyway."

"Because of this?" Nick slapped the paper down on the counter.

"Yes, well, that's one of the reasons."

Nick cocked an eyebrow. "Is that the reason your father called you?"

Jennifer nodded. "He wanted me to be more discreet with my new *friend*."

Nick grinned. "Friend, huh?"

"When I was a teen I rebelled quite a bit. I was a bit of an embarrassment to my family. So I try to avoid the limelight and now this…"

Nick wrapped his arms around her. "This is nothing. Those pictures are an invasion of privacy."

"You're not mad?"

"No, why would I be mad?"

"I'm confused. Why are you here, then?"

"I was worried about you. You just disappeared after your shift. I thought we were going to do something or at least talk, but you were gone."

"I had to get out of there." Jennifer switched off the kettle, which had begun to wail. "I thought you would be mad about the photographs."

"I'm not thrilled, but really, there's nothing I can do, nothing we can do. You can't stop living your life because of it."

Jennifer pushed out of his arms. "I don't like to be humiliated. I don't like the attention."

"So you've said."

"Maybe that makes me a bit of a lone wolf, too."

Nick chuckled. "It's not a bad thing. Why did you run today? Was it because of David? What did he say to you on the podium?"

"He irks me and it's not just the jilting." She took a deep breath. She hadn't told Nick about the research, because it was a secret shame she carried. How she'd been duped by the man she'd loved, how hours of her life researching dissecting aortic aneurysms had all been for naught because it had been claimed by Dr. Morgan.

"David and I worked together on his breakthrough research. He stole my work after he publicly humiliated me."

Nick frowned. "There was no way to sue him?"

Jennifer shook her head. "No, because we were supposed to be getting married. I...I thought we'd share it and then we didn't get married, but by then it was too late."

"Bastard." Nick smiled at her. "Look, I understand about running away from problems, I do. But don't let him get to you. You're better than him."

Jennifer nodded. "I know. Honestly, I thought you'd never want to be around me again because of those pictures. They were taken on your property at Lake Tahoe, Nick."

"That's not your fault. You didn't know. If you knew and they were in cahoots with you, yeah, I might be a little ticked, but you didn't know. It's not your fault."

"What if they find out about your past?"

Nick's smile disappeared. "Ah...well, that's a bit different."

"See, you're better off without me." She turned away, but he spun her around, his eyes intense and locked on her.

"I decide who's good for me or not." And as if to prove something to her, he pulled her against his body and kissed her for all he was worth. The kiss was even better than the first two times they'd kissed.

It was urgent, passionate. Like he was staking his claim.

When it ended, she leaned her head against his shoulder, his arms around her. "I can't get hurt again. I can't let anyone humiliate me again."

"I won't ever do that to you."

Jennifer's heart skipped a beat. She wanted to believe him, but David had shattered her trust in all men completely. She just didn't know what to believe anymore.

All she knew, all she wanted was to feel.

She wanted Nick to make her forget this day. She didn't want to think about the headlines or using discretion. With him, she felt like her old self. Carefree.

Nick helped her forget.

She didn't want to pretend to be this perfect

person anymore. She didn't want to hide. All she wanted right here and right now was Nick.

Jennifer took his hand and pulled him toward the stairs.

"Jennifer, are you sure?" he asked.

"More than sure." She kissed him again, running her fingers through his hair and down his neck. "Just one more night."

She just wanted one more night with Nick. Even if their relationship didn't work out in the long run, she needed him at this moment. Nick was stable, he was a constant, someone she could cling to. Someone who saw her and understood her.

"Please, make love to me, Nick."

"Jennifer," he whispered, stroking her face.

"Please."

Nick scooped her up in his arms. Her arms came around his neck, tangling in the hair at the nape of his neck. He carried her to her room, to her bed.

No words were needed as he moved up the steps. He set her down on her feet in front of him.

"You're so beautiful," he murmured as he

cupped her face with his hands. He pressed his lips against her and she melted into him.

The last time they'd been together it had been fast, hot and heavy. This time she wanted to take things slowly with him.

Nick let his hands drift from her cheeks down to her shoulders and where her simple white cotton nightgown was held up by two ties. He pushed her satin housecoat off and then pulled on the ties of her nightgown.

She let out a moan and bit her lip, thinking about what would come next, about him possessing her. Nick made her burn, in the best way possible.

"What's wrong?" he asked.

"Nothing, I just… Nick, I can't get enough of you."

Nick's eyes sparkled in the darkness and she kissed him again, holding her soft body against his, trying to meld the two of them together.

He undid her nightgown and it fell to the floor. He trailed his mouth down her neck, the flutter of her pulse heating his blood further, and when his kiss traveled down over her breasts, she gasped.

"Did I hurt you?" he murmured against her ear, drinking in the scent of her.

"No." Jennifer moved and sat down on her bed, taking his hand and pulling him closer. "Never."

She reached out and undid his jeans, tugging them down so he was naked. He kicked them off as she reached into a drawer for protection. Ginny had given them to her as a housewarming gag gift when she moved to Las Vegas. At first she'd been scandalized by the prospect, but now she was glad for them. She opened the packet and reached out to touch him.

"Oh, God," he moaned. His body trembled as her hands stroked his abdomen.

He let her pull him down on the bed beside her. They lay down together and he ran his hands over her body slowly. It was torture.

And when he slid her underwear off, she bit her lip. He kissed her again, her legs opening up to welcome his weight. He kept the connection as he entered her. She cried out as he stretched her, filled her completely.

He began to move, her body stretched out beneath him, and he stroked her long, slender neck.

Her nails raked across his back as he increased his speed.

The only sound was their breathing as they moved together as one. Nothing between them. There was no going back for her.

Jennifer groaned as she tightened around his erection, her body releasing as her orgasm moved through her. It didn't take him long before he followed her. He threw back his head, his hands on her hips, holding her tight against him as he came.

She never wanted to let Nick go.

She didn't want to walk away from him again, but she was scared to try. So scared.

"I think…I think I'm falling in love with you."

His body stiffened. "What?"

Jennifer propped herself up on one elbow. "I think I'm falling for you."

Nick sighed. "I thought that's what you said."

She waited for something from him, but he didn't say anything. He just stroked her face. "I don't think you know who you're falling for."

"I know who you were, Nick."

He sat up. "Do you?"

"I know you're a surgeon. I know you're a caring, strong man and were a soldier. One who earned the Medal of Honor—"

"How do you know that?" he asked, agitation in his voice.

"What?"

"How do you know about my medal?"

"I saw it in your drawer the night I stayed over."

Nick cursed under his breath. "You went snooping through my things?"

"I was looking for a towel. I opened the wrong drawer. Why are you hiding it? You should be proud of it."

He snorted. "Proud? I'm not proud of it. It just reminds me of… I'm not proud of it."

"What does it remind you of?"

Nick shook his head. "I have to go." He got up and started pulling on his clothes.

"Don't go."

He paused and sat back down on her bed. "I got that medal for saving Marc's and another man's lives. The army honored me when I didn't deserve it. Marc is paralyzed because of me."

"He's not paralyzed because of you! He's paralyzed because of an IED explosion." Jennifer pulled him closer. "He didn't have to go after you."

"He's my brother. He's always protected me, always gotten me out of stupid jams that I got myself into."

"And he's an adult. He didn't have to follow you. You have to stop blaming yourself."

"I should go," he mumbled.

"No, I'm sorry. Just stay. Stay with me."

Nick nodded and they lay back down together. She curled up against him, listening to his heartbeat.

She was falling hard and fast for him, but she also felt like one wrong move and he might just bolt.

Nick stayed only until she fell asleep. It was still dark out, but dawn would be coming soon. He put on his clothes and left her home. He was hoping no paparazzi were out there, lurking, but only for her sake.

Jennifer put on this brave front, but she was scared of being hurt again. She was just as scared as he was. He was terrified of hurting someone he loved again, of driving a wedge between himself and that person, of having yet another person in his life not talking to him.

And he didn't want Jennifer not talking to him. He didn't want that wedge between them. For the first time in a long time he'd felt like himself again. Not a zombie, not someone living and going through the motions.

He wasn't alone anymore. Yeah, he thought of himself as a lone wolf, but that's not what he wanted.

He missed the camaraderie of the other medics. He missed his brother.

He missed being able to pick up a phone and talk to Marc about anything. Marc would always have the answer; he'd always know what to say to put him at ease.

The silence between them had been going on too long for him. Yet he'd sworn to Marc that he would keep his distance, that he wouldn't interfere in his life. It's why he'd left Chicago, left all his friends behind to come to Nevada.

He was in exile, in self-imposed solitary confinement, and he certainly didn't deserve Jennifer, but he was so glad she was there.

The moment he'd realized she'd left the hospital he'd known why. He'd seen the headlines, just like he'd seen them the night they'd saved that man's life at The Bank nightclub. It must be horrible to live under such a microscope.

Even though her father rode her hard about being a black sheep or whatever, at least her family hadn't cut her off, like his had.

She could be your family if you wanted her to be.

Only he wasn't sure that he deserved that. Though he longed for it.

He'd bought the cabin up at Lake Tahoe to be an income property, but the more time he spent there, the more he pictured kids and a wife and, yeah, even Rufus running around and enjoying the great outdoors.

He had the double-wide trailer and numerous bedrooms and though he'd sworn to himself that he would flip it, he couldn't help but picture the same scenarios in his head as he walked through each and every empty room.

Now those fantasies included Jennifer and a life with her because, try as he might, he couldn't deny it. He loved her.

Of course, those were all just fantasies he'd

had, but now it could be so easy to have everything he'd ever wanted with her, but he was too afraid to try.

CHAPTER FOURTEEN

"Excellent work, Dr. Harvey," Nick said as he began to close the incision site made by the All Saints cardiothoracic attending on call. He'd been working another long shift in the ER when a dissecting aortic aneurysm had been brought in.

"Thank you, Dr. Rousseau. I'm surprised you called me, though, I thought all these cases were to be taken care of by Dr. Morgan." There was a hint of censure in Dr. Harvey's voice and Nick couldn't blame him.

In the two weeks Dr. Morgan had been here, he'd been prancing around the hospital and barking at the trauma staff like he owned the place. Nick didn't understand how someone like Jennifer could've fallen for a creep like David Morgan, but that was just his opinion and he was a bit biased.

"Well, I have a feeling Dr. Morgan isn't an on-call specialist."

Dr. Harvey snickered behind his mask. "Doesn't Dr. Morgan know that most of the dissections I've seen in my career in Las Vegas happen at night? People think it's a bad case of heartburn; they ignore it all day until at night when it gets unbearable. You'd think a cardiothoracic surgeon, especially one studying dissecting aortic aneurysms, would know that."

"I saw the same thing overseas during my service. Nighttime was when soldiers would be brought in." Usually it was uncontrolled blood pressure in a high-stress environment that would bring it about. He hadn't seen many, but he'd seen enough.

"Ah, yes, you served overseas as a medic. Stress-induced, I suppose?" Dr. Harvey asked.

"Yes, because every soldier gets a physical before heading overseas."

"Maybe you should be conducting his trial." Dr. Harvey laughed, but Nick didn't join in. He was just a simple meatballer. He didn't have aspirations of medical trials or surgical breakthroughs.

Why not?

"Good job to you as well, Dr. Rousseau. Can I leave you to finish up?" Dr. Harvey asked.

"Of course. Thank you for your help."

Dr. Harvey nodded and stepped away from the surgical field, heading toward the scrub room. Nick finished closing the patient, and when he was done, he left it to the nurses to get the patient up to the ICU because the man had a rough recovery ahead. He peeled off the surgical gown and tossed it in the hamper and disposed of the gloves and mask.

The door to the scrub room opened as he washed his hands, but Nick didn't look up. He was too tired to care who it was.

"I heard you repaired a dissection in here."

"Yes, Dr. Morgan. Dr. Harvey and I repaired a dissection."

David shut the scrub-room door. "Why wasn't I paged?"

"You were," Nick said. "You were at dinner, or so you told the charge desk."

David's eyes narrowed. "She didn't tell me it was a type-A dissection."

"When she called you, we were still doing the

scans." Nick picked up the bar of soap. "Time is of the essence in cases like this."

"I'm well aware of the histology in cases like this," David snapped.

"Then you should've raced over here instead of finishing your steak." Nick rinsed his hands and then toweled them off.

"How dare you?"

Nick snorted. "What? Save a man's life?"

"This is my *field*. I'm the one to be consulted."

"As I said, you were called. Perhaps you should set up camp here in the hospital for the remainder of your time here—that way you can get to the dissections as they come in." Nick didn't have time to waste on this arrogant moron.

A bully. That's what he was.

"Here's the patient's chart, Dr. Rousseau." The scrub nurse was looking at them, surprised.

"Thank you, Nurse Smith." Nick took the chart and tucked it under his arm. "If you'll excuse me, I have a surgical report to prepare and a family to speak to."

Nick tried to walk by, but David stood in his way.

"Next time, you will wait for me."

"And let someone die while you take your time getting to the hospital? I'm sorry, but that's not how I practice medicine." Nick pushed him out of the way and left the scrub room, hoping that would be the end of it, but he wasn't so sure.

David didn't seem like the type of guy who gave up. He was the type of guy who was catered to and schmoozed. People did what he wanted, when he wanted. David was a real snake in the grass and Nick was sure, because he'd stood up to him, that David wasn't finished with him. Not by a long shot. But he didn't care.

He headed for the trauma floor to finish his charting and do his report in one of the new offices designated for just that purpose, since he didn't have his own office, and just as he'd feared, he heard quick footsteps behind him.

Nick didn't acknowledge David as he fell into step beside him.

"I don't think we'd finished our conversation back there, Dr. Rousseau."

Nick feigned surprise. "Really? Because I was certain we had."

Watch your temper. The temper was what always drove him to take out a bully. Usually he was pretty easygoing, but if someone rubbed him the wrong way and pushed him too far, he'd snap, and he didn't really want to punch David out in the hospital and humiliate Jennifer further.

She'd made it clear the other night how she felt about it.

They'd managed to evade the press and act more discreetly.

It was better this way. He could take it slowly with her. No one would get hurt.

"Oh, we're not done, Rousseau. Not by a long shot," David hissed in his ear, before grabbing him aggressively and pushing him back.

"What is your problem?" Nick snapped. "You were called, you didn't respond and the man will live. I say that's win-win, wouldn't you, Doctor?"

David's eyes narrowed. "Oh, don't give me that. I should have you fired for not having me priority paged."

"What do you want from me, Dr. Morgan? Do you want an apology? If that's the case, one will not be forthcoming."

David sneered. "Is that so? Well, I think in your case some apologies are in order."

"What the hell are you talking about?"

David leaned closer. "I know all about your brother and his *accident*. I also know you have a bit of a temper. Are you going to smash any more windows, Dr. Rousseau? That would *really* embarrass your girlfriend."

Nick counted to ten in his head.

"I have no idea what you're talking about." Nick really wanted to tell him where to go, but he'd promised Jennifer he'd behave. He'd promised her that he wouldn't embarrass her ever.

"Oh, come, Dr. Rousseau. Your act of valor was well publicized, but others don't speak so highly of you. Your brother, for instance, called you reckless."

"You've talked to my brother?"

David smirked. "Once. He mentioned he had a reckless, thoughtless and careless brother. Isn't that why Dr. Marc Rousseau is in a chair, because your impulsiveness got the better of you and your brother ran in to clean up the mess?"

It was like a knife to the gut. David was baiting him. He wanted a fight and Nick knew then without a shadow of a doubt it had nothing to do with dissections or saving a man's life. Hell, it didn't even have anything to do with his *precious* research. It was Jennifer. Plain and simple.

David was jealous that he'd been with Jennifer, or, even more perturbing, David wanted Jennifer back, and if that was the case, there was no way in hell Nick was going to stand aside and allow that.

Nick froze and stared at David, his pulse thundering in his ears and anger threatening to overtake him. "Tread carefully."

"Is that a threat?"

"Take it how you want." Nick watched him and counted in his head, trying to keep himself in check, but the urge to knock the guy out was a battle he was losing.

"I'll have you fired for noncompliance."

"You think the board will fire me for saving a man's life? Because I don't think that will happen. I'm a damn good trauma surgeon and I'm done bandying words with you. If you know what's good for you, you'll stay out of my way, Dr. Morgan."

"Oh, of course you think your *precious* position here is safe. It's because you're sleeping with the head of trauma. Tell me, Rousseau, does it make you feel good about yourself and your failed career in the army to be doing your boss? Does it make you feel like a bigger man?"

Nick pulled back his fist and plowed it into David's face, knocking the surgeon out cold in the middle of the new trauma department.

It had been all he could do to contain his anger, but the man had kept pushing him. It had been bad enough the bastard had talked bad about his brother, but to say things about Jennifer… It had driven him over the edge. He'd managed to keep that reckless, unpredictable side of himself hidden and locked away for so long, but it was just like when he'd run out to save his friend from the IED explosion and when he'd smashed his hand into the window. He'd acted before he'd thought.

"Dammit," he cursed under his breath, shaking his hand, which stung, and then he realized everyone in the trauma department had stopped what they were doing. Everyone was looking at them, and as he turned around, he saw Jennifer standing there and behind her was a group of reporters, who were furiously taking pictures.

"Nick, how could you?" Jennifer wasn't blushing, but he could tell she felt mortified. She walked past him and knelt down beside David. "Someone get a stretcher."

Seeing her on the floor, tending to her ex, caused a pang of jealousy to flood through him and he didn't like feeling this way. He didn't like becoming this irresponsible person again.

"Jennifer, I—"

She held up her hand. "I don't want to hear it."

Two other doctors helped Dr. Morgan to his feet and got him on a stretcher, where he was moaning. Nick stood there, trying to get his anger in check.

"Take him to a private trauma room," Jennifer whispered to the other attendings.

"Jennifer, I can explain."

"Not now, Nick. Not now, and I think it's best you go home for the night." She couldn't look him in the eye as she moved past him and tried to usher the press out of the area.

Nick cursed under his breath and picked up the discarded chart, handing it to a nurse. "Have Dr. Harvey finish the operative report and inform the family of Mr. Berlin's progress."

"Yes, Dr. Rousseau." Even the nurse couldn't look him in the eyes as she took the chart. Nick glanced down at his fist. His knuckles were bloody and bruised, but that wasn't what hurt most.

He was ashamed he'd hurt Jennifer. Embarrassed her and ruined something good. He ruined everything good in his life.

He was bad news and he had to get out of the hospital before he embarrassed her further. How could he expect to have any kind of life with Jennifer when every personal relationship he had was strained? When the people he loved ostracized him?

And he wanted Jennifer.

He loved her.

Nick was tired of being alone, but the only way he could face the future was to face the ghosts of his past, and he wasn't sure he was ready to do that, but he was going to try.

First, though, he had to make a phone call.

"Jennifer?" It was a pitiful moan.

Jennifer tried not to roll her eyes as David came to. There was a secret satisfaction seeing his face with a big red mark across his cheek.

There were a few times she'd wanted to slug him; she just hadn't had the guts.

"Yes."

He smiled and reached out for her, but she didn't take his outstretched hand. She stepped back from him and crossed her arms.

"What's wrong?"

"I don't know why you're looking to me for comfort," Jennifer said. "Last time I checked, you'd married Rita after leaving me at the altar."

David sighed loudly. "Are you still on that? That was two years ago. Can you live and let live?"

"Do you want me to call your wife to come and comfort you?" She cocked her head. "Although I see you're not wearing your wedding ring."

His face turned red. "I took it off while I was doing surgery."

She didn't believe him. Not one bit. "Right."

"Fine, my marriage is over. It didn't last."

"That doesn't surprise me."

David sat up. "I was a fool to leave you. That's why I chose All Saints in Las Vegas. I've come to see if there's a chance for us."

When her heart had first been broken, Jennifer

had often thought of this moment happening, but now she didn't want this. She didn't want David anymore. Maybe she never had.

All she wanted was Nick.

She'd told him the other night that she thought she was falling for him, but really she'd already fallen. She was in love with him.

"There isn't a chance for us, David. And I realize now how painfully we're not suited to each other. I'm sorry you chose All Saints on the foolish notion that I would fall back into your arms again, but I'm not interested. I'm here to do my job."

"It's because of that Dr. Rousseau fellow, isn't it?"

"Dr. Rousseau has nothing to do with my decision not to give us another chance."

David's lip curled. "Doesn't it? I saw the headlines. You romping around Las Vegas with him like some kind of tramp."

Jennifer took a deep breath. Now she was beginning to get an inkling of why Nick had clobbered him. "Going on a date doesn't make me a tramp. Cheating on a wife or a fiancée makes you a tramp and, David, you're a big one."

He rolled his eyes. "Did you just call me a whore?"

Jennifer grinned. "I believe I did."

"I made a mistake, coming here." David shook his head.

"You sure did. Now I want you to tell me what the heck happened. Why did Nick feel the need to punch you out in the middle of my trauma department?"

David sat up slowly, rubbing the side of his jaw. "He instigated it."

"I highly doubt it."

"Come on, Jennifer. If you only knew what kind of person he was—"

She held up her hand. "I don't care what kind of person he was before. Dr. Morgan, I'm going to recommend your program be removed from my trauma department."

"Dr. Ramsgate won't go for that. Do you know how much prestige I bring with me? I'm a cardiothoracic god."

Jennifer took a step closer and gave him the stare down, and from the wide-eyed expression on his face, she could tell it wasn't amusing him like it had amused Nick. It was having the desired effect.

"You're going to leave my hospital. You're going to do it peacefully and quietly. I don't care what *damn* excuse you use, but you're going to leave."

"Is that a threat?"

"Damn straight. I have papers proving how much I assisted in your 'solo' breakthrough research. I held off trying to put my name on it because I was hurt and embarrassed, but now I don't care anymore. I'm not embarrassed. I don't care how it'll affect my father's presidential campaign. If you don't want me raising a stink about stolen work, I suggest you find another place to continue your trial."

David paled. The threat had worked. She'd never in a million years do such a thing normally, but she would if it meant getting David out of her hospital. She didn't want to see him again. She was over him, way over, and she wasn't going to be ashamed about her past any longer.

"That's blackmail."

"Take it as you will." She smiled at him. "You have forty-eight hours to get out of my face."

She turned and left the room, shutting the door and drowning out the sounds of his curses. It would work, and if he went to the press or the board, she had the paperwork, the proof that she should be credited, and if there was one thing about David that she knew, he didn't like sharing the spotlight.

Jennifer knew her father wouldn't be pleased with her, or about the scene caused today, but she didn't care. His election wouldn't be hurt by it. Far from it, and maybe for once it would show Dr. Morgan in a bad light.

Yeah, the fight had mortified her, until she'd realized what it was about. Nick had been standing up for her honor and she'd dismissed him. The hurt on his face made her heart ache.

She never wanted to hurt Nick.

As soon as her shift was over she was going to make things right by him. She was going to tell him how she felt.

She was going to tell him she loved him.

She was going to open her heart one more time and take a risk, a chance on love. Even if it meant her heart would be broken again.

Living without love wasn't something she wanted.

She wanted so much more.

She wanted Nick.

Now she just had to break it to her father that there would be some headlines about her and two surgeons fighting over her.

Jennifer smiled as she pulled out her phone and dialed.

Rufus just wagged his tail politely as Nick slammed the door behind him.

"Sorry, pal." Nick set his keys down next to the phone.

Call him.

Sweat broke across his brow as he thought of Marc. Of his family.

Call him.

He wanted to. He wanted to apologize and make things right, even if it fell on deaf ears.

He had to do this if he wanted to move on.

Talking to Marc would probably never ease the guilt, but it would give him closure and maybe then he could move on.

He picked up the phone and switched it on. The dial tone sounded loud. Too loud. He switched it off, cursing under his breath.

I can't do this.

Marc was better off without him. His family was better off without him. Jennifer was better off. And when he thought of Jennifer living without him, it tore at his heart.

That's not what he wanted.

If she could face David, he could face his own demons. Nick switched on the phone and, as if on autopilot, dialed the eleven digits he knew so well.

It rang twice and his pulse thundered in his ears.

"Hello?" the familiar voice answered. One he'd missed. Nick didn't say anything. He couldn't.

"Hello?" Marc sounded annoyed. "Who's there?"

It was now or never, and if he didn't do this, how could he ever be with Jennifer?

Quite simply, he couldn't.

"Who's there? I can hear you breathing."

"Marc, it's me. Nick."

There was silence on the other end and Nick couldn't help but wonder if he'd made a horrible mistake. Maybe their father had been right. Perhaps he should've kept away.

"Nick?" Marc didn't ask this question in anger,

more like in shock with a hint of hope. "Is that really you?"

"Yeah," Nick said. "It's been a long time."

"I'll say. Where the heck have you been?"

"Nevada."

"Nevada? Why are you there? I thought you were going to come back to Chicago when your tour of duty was done."

"I wanted to give you space. I know that you blamed me for what happened to you."

There was silence again and muttered curses under his breath. "Who told you that?"

"Dad."

Now the cursing was louder. "I'm not mad at you, Nick."

Nick didn't believe him. How could he not be mad at him? "Marc, I paralyzed you."

"You didn't paralyze me, Nick. An IED explosion did."

"But it was my fault. I was reckless and my running out there to save someone cost you."

Marc sighed. "I know. I was ticked you lived 'e so recklessly. I won't deny that. I thought 't it over and over again when I realized I'd never walk again, but I didn't have to run after you. That was me. Not you."

A surge of emotions washed through Nick and he scrubbed a hand over his face. "So you're really not mad?"

"No, you idiot," Marc said, with a slight laugh. "I just didn't know where you went after your tour of duty ended and was working through stuff of my own."

Nick chuckled. "I've been a fool."

"Yeah, we both have been."

Nick didn't say anything else, but his heart was very full. For the first time in a long time he felt whole again. He could finally move forward. There were countless roads of opportunity.

"So," Marc said, breaking the silence. "You're in Vegas?"

"I am."

"Seen any good shows?"

Nick laughed and launched into an easy conversation with his brother, as if they'd never been parted. All that time when he'd thought he'd never see his brother again, when he'd felt less than worthless was washed away. He'd been given a clean slate, a second chance. At every-thing.

And this time he wasn't going to blow it.

CHAPTER FIFTEEN

JENNIFER STOOD IN the middle of the new trauma department. She hadn't seen Nick in two days. After he'd gone home, he'd taken personal leave for a few days. She'd gone by his place, but no one had been home. Even Rufus was gone and she knew he'd retreated up to Lake Tahoe.

He'd needed space.

She just hoped she hadn't blown her chances with him.

When he was gone, she missed him.

She missed the joking, the stolen looks and the understanding. He got her like no one had ever done.

He even let her tell him stupid knock-knock jokes.

David had left the hospital, claiming that a new position had come up at Boston Mercy and he'd accepted. Dr. Ramsgate had been disappointed, and even though the press had splashed the quarrel across the front pages, Jennifer had smoothed it over.

Dr. Harvey and she had explained the reason for the fight and the board was on Nick's side. He'd done all that was required of him and Dr. Morgan hadn't been available to do the surgery. The utmost importance was the patient's life.

The transition to the new trauma department had gone smoothly and the old trauma wing was being turned into a walk-in clinic with a hefty pro-bono grant from Senator Mills.

Everything was falling into place. Except Nick.

She sighed and started to walk over to the old trauma department, where she was overseeing plans to turn it into the walk-in clinic, and as she walked down the once bustling hallway she was surprised to see a man in dark denim and leather leaning against the wall.

It took her a moment to realize she was staring at Nick in his street clothes.

"Do you have a moment?" he asked.

"Of course."

"Good, let's go outside." Nick turned and walked to the old ER doors, pushing them open, and Jennifer followed him outside, squinting as her eyes adjusted to the bright sunshine.

"Working a night shift?" he asked.

"Yes," she said, and then chuckled. "I've been pulling a lot of all-nighters the last couple of days."

Nick nodded and they took a seat on a park bench overlooking the strip. "Look, I wanted to say I'm sorry about what happened. I didn't mean to humiliate you in front of the press like that."

"There's no need to apologize—"

"No, let me finish."

She nodded. "Okay."

Nick scrubbed his hands over his face. "I didn't ever want to hurt you. My whole life I've seemed to screw up relationships with the people I care about and you walked back into my life and…"

Jennifer reached out and touched his leg. "I get it."

Nick nodded. "You do. You do get me. You see me."

"I do," she whispered. "Just like you see me."

He shook his head. "Only I don't. You asked me not to humiliate you, you told me how terrified you were of the press, and then I punch out that…well, and I punched out David."

"I know." She smiled.

Nick winced. "Right, you were there."

"I was and it doesn't matter."

"It does, because I said I would never humiliate you and I did just that."

"You didn't humiliate me. You gave me freedom."

Nick smiled. "I love you, Jennifer."

Her heart leapt, hearing the words. It was hard to believe and if it wasn't for the fact the sun was beating down on her and making her sweat, she might've believed she was dreaming. This was the last thing she'd been expecting from him. "You love me?"

Nick nodded. "I didn't think I could ever love someone as much as I love you. I didn't think I deserved to love someone. Not when I couldn't even forgive or love myself."

"Oh, Nick. You didn't paralyze Marc. An IED did."

"I did. He ran after me. Everyone told me not to go out there and rescue my comrade but I did anyway and Marc…he was coming to my rescue like always and paid the price I should've paid."

Jennifer slid closer to him. "It wasn't your fault. You did a heroic thing, don't blame yourself."

"I couldn't forgive myself until I had Marc's forgiveness and I was trying to give him distance. Trying to fade from his life, but that wasn't right. So I called him."

"And what did he say?"

"He reamed me out for not calling him sooner." Nick smiled. "We worked it out. I think, in time, I'll have my brother back. It's going to take some healing, but…yeah."

Jennifer squeezed his knee. "I'm so happy for you."

"As for David, I'll try to work with him. I swear there will be no more fights in the trauma department."

"Don't worry about Dr. Morgan. He's gone."

Nick was confused. "How?"

"I blackmailed him." She laughed when she saw his wide-eyed expression.

"What do you mean, you blackmailed him? You? Blackmailed him?"

"Is that so hard to believe?" she teased.

"It is, actually. That's kind of scary. How?"

"I threatened to sue him for stealing my part of his precious research if he didn't leave the hospital, and he wasn't to tell anyone that I coerced him into leaving or that it was your fault. I have all the paperwork to prove the theft. Well, I did. He took it, just to make sure I didn't go back on my word."

Nick chuckled. "I can't believe you did that. That's… Wow."

"Changing your mind about me?" She winked.

"Never. So why did he come here?"

"He didn't come here for research. He came here to try and get back together with me."

"I thought so." Nick went very quiet.

"I turned him down. I don't want to get back together with David. I was blind last time. I thought I was in love, but it wasn't love. I've never loved him. The man I love is you, Nick."

"What…what did you say?"

"I said I love you, too. I'm not just falling for you. I already fell for you. Long ago, probably when you put up with my stupid joke."

He beamed, but then the smile disappeared.

"What about your father? I'm not exactly his idea of a good choice."

"I don't care. He never approved of anyone except David, and look how that turned out." Jennifer snorted. "My dad is not the best judge of men."

"And you are?" Nick teased.

She smiled and moved toward him, her heart racing. "I'd like to think so."

An answering smile spread across his face. "Really?"

"I do. I came here to escape my ghosts and swore that I would never ever get involved with another surgeon, but then you were here and… I held onto the memory of you for so long. That one perfect night. I didn't think it could get any better and I was scared to try, but you worked your way in and I'm so glad you did."

Nick reached out and pulled her against him, kissing her, and she wished they weren't sitting on a park bench out in front of a hospital. She wanted to seal the deal skin on skin, in his bed or her bed. She didn't care which.

All she wanted was Nick, and she was willing to risk her heart again to have that.

"I love you, Jennifer. I do." Nick ran his thumbs over her cheeks, his hazel eyes twinkling. "I love you so much."

Jennifer stroked his cheek. "I'm willing to try again, Nick, and I'm willing to try with you. Just don't break my heart or I'll slug you."

Nick grinned. "Deal." He pulled her back into a kiss that melted her into a pile of goo and she didn't give a damn that someone might be lurking in the bushes, taking pictures.

She'd found love. Real love, and this time there would be no running away.

This time, she was never going to let him go.

EPILOGUE

One year later

JENNIFER WANDERED OUT of Nick's cabin, which had been updated to include a more modern bathroom. As she walked across the deck, Rufus raised his head and wagged his tail at her approach. She reached down and gave him a pet.

The sun was setting over the lake and it reminded her of her first night here.

Except now they didn't have to rush home the next day—they had the week off, and this time she had a toothbrush and a change of clothes.

Her father's campaign had been unsuccessful and he'd finally taken it as a sign to retire from the world of politics. He'd bought a ranch again, just as a hobby farm, outside Carson City, where they raised horses this time instead of dust bunnies and failed crops.

Though there was talk her father was going to

run for mayor of Carson City again, but, then, who knew with him? Her father liked the limelight.

She took a sip of wine and sighed happily. She loved Tahoe and she loved it that this was just her and Nick's spot. No one else came up here, well, except Rufus.

She just wished Nick would get back here so they could enjoy this sunset together. He'd gone to town over two hours ago and he hadn't told her why.

"He's a dead man, you know that, right?" she said to Rufus. Rufus responded with a happy pant and then got up and trotted across the deck. "Where are you go…?" She trailed off when she realized Nick was standing in the doorway, wearing his old uniform.

"Did you reenlist or something?"

"No, I just thought that I would do what I'm about to do right. I thought I'd wear what I was wearing that first night I saw you."

Jennifer paused. "Wait. What?"

Nick chuckled and walked over to meet her. He looked so damn fine in that uniform. She'd forgotten how good he looked. And then he got down on one knee and her own knees buckled.

"What're you doing?"

Nick smiled, his hazel eyes twinkling. "I think it's pretty obvious. Jennifer, will you marry me?" And then he held out a ring.

She didn't even have to think. She knew. "Yes."

He grinned and stood up, slipping the ring on her finger and then pulling her close. "Good. I didn't want to have to lock you up here until you agreed."

"You're a dingbat." She glanced down at her hand. "You know my father will want to plan the wedding. Some big lavish affair."

Nick shrugged. "If that's what you want."

"No, I don't. How about we get married today?"

"What?"

"We're in Tahoe. In Nevada. Let's do it."

Nick shook his head. "My brother will say it's irresponsible."

"I doubt that."

Jennifer grinned at the look of shock on Nick's face when he turned round to see his brother Marc wheeling himself onto the deck. His girlfriend, Anne, followed him, both of them grinning.

"What are you doing here?" Nick asked in disbelief, walking over to his brother to take his hand.

"Your…well, I guess your fiancée flew us down from Chicago as a surprise." Marc winked at Jennifer.

Nick turned back. "You flew them down?"

Jennifer shrugged. "You two talk on the phone, but you know doctors and their work schedules—everyone is too busy all the time. So I arranged it."

Nick kissed her quickly. "Thank you."

"You've got quite a woman there. Don't screw this up," Marc teased.

Nick laughed. "I won't. I swear."

"So? Do we go get married now or wait until the morning?" Jennifer said.

"You're serious? I thought you were kidding."

Nick kissed her, passionately, just like he had that first time, and it made her forget everything, except taking him upstairs to their bed, but they couldn't do that with their guests there.

Suddenly getting married right at this moment didn't seem like such a good idea. The only thought she had in her mind now was getting to know her new family. The wedding chapel would be there tomorrow.

"No, we'll wait until tomorrow. That's the responsible thing," Jennifer conceded. "How about we all have a nice dinner and some wine?"

"Sounds good to me!" Anne said. "Come on, Marc, let's finish unpacking."

Marc and Anne headed back into the cabin.

"I can't believe you brought him here," Nick said in disbelief.

"Think of it as an engagement gift." She kissed him again. "I love you and if you ever hurt me, I'll fire you!"

Nick laughed and then picked her up. "You're the boss."

* * * * *

MILLS & BOON®
Large Print Medical

October

November

December

MILLS & BOON®
Large Print Medical

January

February

March